CHANGE OF PACE

Sharon Brondos

A KISMET™ Romance

 METEOR PUBLISHING CORPORATION

Bensalem, Pennsylvania

KISMET™ is a trademark of Meteor Publishing Corporation

First Printing August 1990.

ISBN: 1-878702-05-X

To Pat Dalton

SHARON BRONDOS

Sharon Brondos has been writing professionally since 1982. She holds a masters degree in Asian History. Sharon lives in Casper, Wyoming with her husband, Greg. Her three children are now in college. She is the author of nine published romances, as well as numerous published poems and short fiction.

ONE

Deirdre Wilcox crossed her legs, feeling the silky nylon slide along her thighs and shins as she readjusted her position in the hard wooden chair. The deliberate movement seemed to attract the attention of the man sitting behind the cluttered desk opposite her. But only for a fraction of a moment, making Deirdre feel she was only a minor annoyance to him. Then his green-eyed gaze returned to study the papers she had handed to him, along with some others that lay atop the mess on the wooden desktop.

Why in the world had she allowed herself to be badgered and bullied by her father and her doctor into coming to this godforsaken place, she wondered. And *further*, why had she agreed to take a simple job? One that would give her something to occupy her time while her body rested but would make none of the demands on her which had caused the stress that had made her agree to this plan in the first place!

The policeman to whom she had given her résumé didn't seem any more pleased about the circumstances than she was, she decided. His broad, sculptured features were frowning, the corners of his wide mouth pulled downward, making the cleft on his chin deepen. Deirdre had faced up to some intimidating men in her years acting as her father's hostess. Since her mother's death, she had assumed the duties of the senator's social secretary and had also managed to continue both her education and her part-time job. All *that* had landed her here, facing a man she found far more . . . impressive than anyone she had met in Washington diplomatic circles.

He was big. Really massive, making her feel fragile and almost dainty in her city business suit and heels. But, she decided, it wasn't the broad shoulders and wide chest that made Chief Sam Cassidy so formidable. It was his eyes . . .

Green eyes that seemed to stare right through her. The trained art critic in her tried vainly to lable them with a technical color word, but not even the special training that had enabled her to write her master's thesis on the use of unusual color in American landscapes gave her the language tool to describe adequately those fantastic irises. It wasn't the color alone, either, she realized. It was the spirit of the mind behind them that was getting to her.

"You have an advanced degree in art?" Sam Cassidy's deep voice interrupted her musing. It was the first time since entering the Lodge Pole, Wyoming, police station twenty minutes earlier that she had heard him speak in more than a monosyllable, and the gentleness of his voice surprised her. She had expected more gruffness.

"Art history, to be exact," she replied. "I can't draw a straight line myself, but I do have a critical eye for other people's work." She glanced around the dingy station, noting that the only "art" on the walls were notices, wanted posters, and a calendar with a barely clothed blonde atop it. She saw the chief follow her glance and then cover up what she suspected was a grin with one big hand. A hand crisscrossed with deep red recent scars.

"Well, Miss Wilcox . . ." he said. "It looks as if we're stuck with each other for the duration." He tossed her papers on the desk, and she longed to upbraid him for his sloppiness.

"You could refuse . . ." she began.

Sam Cassidy shook his head. He laced his fingers behind his dark hair and leaned back in the chair. "Fact," he said. "You're out here under doctor's orders. You were trying to be all things to all people, and at the tender age of twenty-six, physiologically, you were starting to blow your cork."

"How did you . . . ?" Deirdre started to rise, anger filling her.

He stood up, causing her to settle back in her seat. "When the governor of this state starts pulling in political favors for the daughter of a Georgia senator," he said, "*I* want to know the reasons. The *real* reasons. I run this town on a thin shoestring, and I need to know that I can depend on the performance and loyalty of my staff. Every one of them."

Deirdre laughed. "Then you couldn't possibly

want to hire me. If you know so much about my background . . .''

The chief made a sudden movement with his scarred hand that created a clear resting place for one lean hip on the side of his desk. ''Your background, Miss Wilcox, shows me that at your age, you've had more experience in dealing with people, protocol, crises, and just plain life than almost anyone I've ever met. I'm only surprised you didn't actually have a breakdown.''

She raised her chin. ''The doctor only discovered the blood pressure and stress symptoms in a routine exam. I could have—''

''Continued on the way you were and gone nuts. Or killed yourself by the time you were thirty.'' He regarded her for a moment. ''And that would have been a terrible waste.''

Sam regretted the last words the moment they left his mouth. When she had walked in the door, it had been all he could do to keep from gaping like a schoolboy. His years in California had accustomed him to seeing beautiful women, but Deirdre Wilcox was special. It wasn't just the long legs, shapely form, blue eyes, and honey-colored hair. The way she carried herself, the poise that stopped just short of arrogance, the . . . wisdom he saw behind the hurt and confusion in those azure eyes. She may have crammed too much into too few years, but the value of her experience was clear to him. This was a woman with intelligence and wisdom far beyond her two-plus decades of life. Probably, he decided, in some ways more than he had acquired in thirty-four, rugged though they had been until he had moved out of the West Coast scene and taken this job in Lodge Pole. Smartest personal move he had ever made.

"Miss Wilcox . . ." he went on, hoping that he could maintain the proper attitude of professionalism after that verbal slip. She hadn't *seemed* to notice, but he had to remind himself of her background. Deirdre Wilcox was trained to cover her emotions and reactions. "Let's not dance this out. You know that your father applied pressure to the governor to find a quiet place and a simple job for you, and that it all ran downhill. I ended up with you on my doorstep, and if I don't let you in—if you don't come in willingly, I'm going to be in deep political . . . trouble. That's just the way it is."

She nodded, her manner cool. But Sam thought he could see clouds of emotion in her eyes. She was accepting, but sure not liking.

"You're right, Chief," she agreed, smoothing the edge of her skirt with a perfectly manicured hand. "It *is* supposed to be for my own good, and I apologize for seeming unpleasant. I appreciate very much that you've considered me for the position."

"You realize that you're incredibly overqualified," he said, the scarred hand running through black hair. "You will find yourself bored from time to time, I'm sure."

Deirdre sighed. "Isn't that the idea? I've got to teach myself to slow down." She gestured, indicating the office *and* the small town beyond. "Isn't this the perfect place to do that?"

Sam Cassidy stood, jamming his hands into the trouser pockets of his western-style police uniform. Deirdre wondered if he had any idea of what an appealing sight he would make to any woman. His features were tanned deeply, with shallow lines running from the corners of his eyes. They were also rugged, rough in a way compared to the smooth-faced career men she had known back East, but handsome in a special "western" way. The uniform, which had to have been hand-tailored to fit the muscular body, added to the appeal. It was traditional police blue, but the pants were jeans and the shirt was yoked and closed by a string tie. A silver star decorated his left chest, and around his waist was strapped a utility belt from which hung a wicked-looking revolver and several cartridge cases. An empty loop, she decided, would hold a nightstick when he patroled. Formidable.

"Don't get the notion that it'll always be quiet," he warned. "It's late May now, but when the tourist season starts in full swing in a couple of weeks, we'll be pulling greenhorns out of ditches, saving them from 'cute' wildlife, keeping them from driving through town at a hundred miles an hour. And, oh yes, there'll be the locals on weekends. Good old boys in town to have fun." He looked down at his big fists. "Can't always count on the mere sight of these to cool some drunk yahoo down."

"Was that how you hurt your hand?" Impulsively, she reached out and touched the scars.

Surprised at the concern, Sam didn't pull away as he would normally have done. Her soft fingertips played over the wounds, soothing them. And sending a slight tingle up his arm.

"No," he answered quietly, hoping that she would continue to touch him. Felt good. "I got this hauling a high-centered truck out of a muddy road a month ago. Cable gave, and I got this."

"Why wasn't a wrecker service . . . ?" The scars were healed, but it was clear to her that he'd have them for the rest of his life.

"Friend of mine. Knew he didn't have the price of a wrecker, so I did it myself." Sam chuckled. "We *did* get the truck out."

Deirdre almost lost her composure. When he smiled, as he was doing for the first time since she had entered the small station, Sam Cassidy suddenly became dazzlingly handsome. The expression erased years and showed a glimmer of a character that wasn't all somber and concerned with "duty." Maybe, she decided, just maybe this man wouldn't be so bad to work for after all. Maybe, before summer was over, they might even be friends. She smiled in return.

"I know how it is, bailing friends out," she said, remembering literally having to do that for some of her more party-prone sorority sisters and then, later, diplomatic acquaintances who had breached local customs in one way or another. Inwardly, she sighed. She was going to miss the excitement of Washington life, even if it was for her own good.

Sam watched her carefully. "You're homesick, aren't you," he said in a kind tone. She might look as sophisticated and beautiful as any woman he'd ever seen, but inside she had to be hurting. Just the fact that she had been forced into "medical leave" showed that she must be the kind of person who was not only personally ambitious, but also gave of herself to others. She must have left droves of friends behind. Maybe even a special man.

She shrugged. "This is all so . . . so different. I'm still in America, I know, but it feels like another *world*."

"I know how you feel." He stared off into space, and Deirdre suddenly realized the color of his eyes was the same shimmery green of the iridescent feathers in a peacock's tail. And that she thought she could see reflected in their depths the same feeling of uprootedness that she was experiencing. Only Sam's pain was far in the past.

"You aren't from here originally?" she asked, her curiosity piqued.

"No." The reply was curt. He turned and went back to his desk chair. "Here's a work contract you have to sign for the city," he said, all business again, leaving her wondering what invisible scar she had managed to touch. She would have sworn that Sam Cassidy was a local. Born and raised in the Wyoming mountains and never set foot out of state. Another miscalculation. She chided herself. Sometimes the simplest of things were the most complex and valuable. That could apply to a person as well.

"So, I'm hired," she stated, drawing back into her role as he had seemed to do.

"I have no choice." His tone had an edge of bitterness. He held out a pen and paper to her.

Anger flared, but she managed to keep it out of her pose. She took the contract and signed it carefully. "I'll do a good job for you, Chief. I've had a lot of experience managing offices."

"And people?" His eyes were green ice.

"People are my specialty." She allowed him a cool smile. "Whether you need someone to organize this . . . place or be a diplomat on the telephone, I'm your woman." She reached out her hand to him.

Sam stared at the hand for a millisecond before taking it in his own. He regretted getting prickly with her, but she had a way of making him want to talk about the past, and that was one thing he didn't care to do. He shook her hand gently, aware of its delicacy in his own rough one. It was like holding a rose, he thought, or a small, beautiful bird. He'd have to be careful—this woman stirred him, and he had only met her this morning.

"All right, Miss Wilcox," he said. "When can you start?"

"Right now, Chief," she said briskly. "What can I throw out?"

Sam released her hand and started to laugh. He'd never been accused of being a pack rat so politely before. She was clearly a politician's daughter. In addition to being the best-looking secretary-dispatcher he'd ever hired, she just might turn out to be the best employee. That reminded him. He'd better warn her about Andy. He had caught the look of disgust on her face at the nudie calendar.

"Well?" She was smiling slightly, obviously moved by his laughter.

"Don't throw anything away," he said. "Just sort it. Until I get a chance to go through it, I won't know what's valuable and what's junk, and I—"

"For heaven's sake, Chief." She spread her arms out. "I don't know how you find the telephone, much less any important papers. Your desk's a disaster." She pointed to a smaller one against a wall that held an ancient manual typewriter. It was also piled with papers. Even the chair had a layer of debris on the seat, and someone had left a down jacket draped on the back. "I take it that's *my* desk. It goes in the same category. *Disaster*. What you need is a fire or a good strong wind to clear things out. I assure you I'll do much less damage if you'll just trust my judgment in—"

"We do get a wind in occasionally," Sam interrupted. Her little tirade had come as close to a dressing-down as he had experienced in a long time, and he didn't like it. "Comes with the climate. As for trusting your judgment, wouldn't that be foolish of me, since we've never worked together?"

She lifted her chin. "I've managed my father's office. I've worked on a dozen political campaigns. I have . . . had a part-time job at the Babcock Gallery. *And* I have an education. I could—"

"I have an education, too, miss." He stood, his hands resting on his desk. "A master's in criminal justice. But when I'm the new kid on the block, I do what the regulars say should be right for the situation. In my line of work, you could get your . . . rear shot off if you didn't listen to someone who's been around."

She only gave him an inch. "If I find a matter totally unrelated to police business, can I toss that?" Her arms were folded defiantly across her chest. Sam wasn't sure whether to smile or frown.

"If it's *totally* unrelated," he conceded. "And that doesn't include Kleenex and toilet paper."

Deirdre started to laugh. "Okay, Chief." She gave

him a smart salute. "I believe I get the message. Can I clean, too? It doesn't look like anyone's done the windows in a decade, much less swept out the dust bunnies. And I think of the bathroom as a chamber of horrors. Where did you get your degrees?"

Her abrupt change of subject caught him unawares. "U.C.L.A. I worked night school while I was on the force. It took . . ." He stopped when he realized that she had tricked him into revealing more of his past. That was gone, a memory better buried for his sake. His life in Lodge Pole was his line to reality, to sanity. "A woman comes in once a week to clean," he said brusquely. "That's not part of your job." He walked over to a machine that sat on a side table.

"This is the dispatch radio," he told her. His forefinger pointed to a switch. "You depress this and just give the call number of whoever's on duty. I'm 'one.' My officer, Andy Davis, is 'two.' Can you remember that?"

"I believe so." She matched his tone in sarcasm. "I've been involved in remote communication on campaigns. But I don't believe I've seen anything quite this old."

"It works. This isn't a wealthy town. Now, I've managed to bully the council out of five dollars an hour for you, but for only eight hours a day. If we have an emergency situation, you'll just have to work for free. Like Andy and I do."

"I can handle that. Who's this Andy?"

Sam smiled mentally. When the two of them confronted, he'd love to be around to see what would happen. Andy, young, blond, and handsome, was an incurable ladies' man, responsible for the only spot of glamour in the room. Besides Deirdre Wilcox, he reminded himself. "He's my one officer," he explained. "We take twelve-hour shifts, but sometimes overlap. The department is just too small to run like a city station with watches and all. Andy and I get along, and I'm sure that after you get to know him, you'll like him, too. Just . . . be a little tolerant at first."

She cocked a honey-colored eyebrow at him. "Of what in particular am I called on to be tolerant, Chief? Is your officer the one who hung that particular bit of chronological pulchritude? Somehow, she doesn't strike me as your type."

"Oh, really?" Sam eased himself down on the cleared spot on the desk again. "And just what do you figure might be my type, Miss Wilcox?"

Deirdre felt an unaccustomed blush in her cheeks. "I don't know," she replied honestly. "But you don't strike me as . . . tacky. I think you just allowed that . . . thing because you like your officer and don't want to offend him."

Sam digested her words. They could be mere flattery, but he expected that they were genuine. "Thanks," he said. "That's true, and I appreciate the fact that you've drawn at least a few positive conclusions about me."

More than a few, she said to herself. Sam Cassidy was a mystery she was determined to unravel during the months they would be working together. Suddenly, she realized for the first time that she was looking forward to the experience instead of thinking of it as an exile from all she loved.

"Tell me more about the radio," she said, feeling a new interest.

"Folks will call in complaints," he said, pointing to the telephone. It was another antique with a dial set in the base. "If Andy or I are in the office, we'll take it ourselves. But if we're on patrol, you'll have to radio us. Lift the switch to receive, depress it to—"

"I know. Do I have to use any special code words, or can I just talk to you in plain English." She sounded impatient.

"Plain English will do fine. We leave the elaborate jargon for the city boys."

She faced him, hands on her hips. "Don't forget, Chief, I'm from the city myself. You don't want to offend your officer? How about trying not to offend me."

He stared at her for a moment. Then: "Fair enough. But I have prejudices, Deirdre. Ones I find hard to leave behind. Please be patient with me and hold on to your temper. I'm afraid I'm highly opinionated, and you're going to need a lot of control at times."

"Warning accepted." She gave him a steady look. "I'll behave publicly. I'm used to that, since my life has always been up for exposure. But if I disagree with you, I intend to speak my mind when we're alone."

Another frown. One which pulled his dark eyebrows down in a furry pucker. "Such a public life," he muttered. "How did you stand it?"

"You learn to live with it. Cultivate the good reporters and try to let what the other kind say run off your shoulders. I was thin-skinned when I was young and used to get really furious when I thought my dad was being poorly treated by the media. But I suppose experience and age have reconciled me to a free press.''

Sam made a low sound in his chest. Then he turned and picked up a nightstick and a small radio receiver. ''I should go out on patrol,'' he said, his voice cold. ''Think you can handle things for an hour or so?''

''Of course.'' *But can* things *handle what I intend to do to them,* she thought wickedly.

TWO

Sam took his hat, a beige Stetson, from the hat rack and shrugged into his windbreaker. The morning had begun sunny and calm, but he knew from experience that it would cloud over and start to blow by lunchtime.

What he didn't know, he reflected as he looked at Deirdre Wilcox's innocent-appearing blue eyes, was what his new secretary was going to be up to in his absence. She was clearly a young woman who was used to having her way. The letter he had received from the governor ''suggesting'' that he hire her for the summer had drawn a picture of a highly competent person who had merely made the mistake of using her energy and competence in too many pies. Lord knew *what* she'd do to the office once he was gone.

Well, he'd have to trust her. That was all. He'd give her an hour, maybe a hair more. Surely she couldn't do much damage in that length of time. He smiled at her, opened the door, and stepped into the morning sunshine, feeling the welcome of the town that had adopted him as its peace officer.

Deirdre stared at the closed door, trying to regain the picture of him smiling. Strong white teeth, emerald eyes that seemed to hold a shadow of fondness, of . . . trust. In the silence and dreary, dust-moted air of the station office, it seemed impossible that his large frame had just occupied space there. Shared it with her. She shook herself to pull herself back to reality.

She had a job! Looking around the room, she felt energy flowing into her veins. She took off her jacket and hung it on the coat rack where his windbreaker had been. Then she rolled up the sleeves of her lilac silk blouse.

Getting out the phone book, she dialed the number of the supermarket and ordered a collection of cleaning supplies, telling the startled manager that she would pay for them on delivery *in cash* if he would get them to the station in ten minutes. Cleaning woman or not, this place needed a good going-over, she thought. No way was she going to sit at the desk, waiting for the phone to ring while all this grime lay around her. Hanging up the phone, she did some quick exploration.

Besides the office, there was one jail cell behind a heavy door. It was unlocked and unoccupied, but it gave her a strange feeling to look inside, knowing that at some point during her term here, it probably would be occupied. It smelled stale, and she put it third on the list after the office and the bathroom. She then went in search of that.

To her relief, the small dark room wasn't as filthy as she had feared. With two men using the place, she had expected a real challenge. But, she thought irreverently, it seemed both policemen had good aim. A knock on the door brought her running down the short hall to let in a stockboy from the store.

She took the cleaning supplies, paid for them, and then told him that there would be a five-dollar tip for him if he could sneak her about a dozen large cardboard boxes. "I need them for storage," she explained to the puzzled youth.

He scratched a thatch of brown hair. "Chief's not moving out, is he?" he asked, his tone concerned.

"No. I'm just . . . organizing a few things." Deirdre was puzzled at the kid's attitude. Everywhere else she had lived, police and teens were sworn enemies. But this young man seemed to feel differently.

"Good." He grinned. "I'd hate to see the Angel leave Lodge Pole. Especially this time of year."

"Angel?"

"Yes, ma'am." The boy's cheeks reddened. "That's what we all call him. The Guardian Angel. You're his girlfriend, aren't you? Why didn't you know that?"

"Because I'm his secretary, and I just met him," Deirdre replied. She gestured with her hand. "Give me a little more. Why the impressive nickname?"

"Gee." He looked even more embarrassed. "I'm sorry, ma'am. I mean, with you dressed so nice and looking so pretty, I just naturally thought you was somebody he knew from his old home. He's sure been a loner since he came here. We all figured he was just waiting to send for . . . somebody like you."

"I'm Deirdre Wilcox," she said, extending her hand. "I'm spending the summer up in Senator Thorton's summer place and working as the chief's secretary. As I said, we just met."

The boy hesit: ', then wiped his palm on his jeans and took her hand. "I'm Tommy Edwards," he said. "I'll get on those boxes right away, ma'am. And you don't need to tip me none."

Deirdre tightened her grip. "Why the nickname, Tommy."

"Oh, he'd be ticked at me if I went and told you." He tried to pull away, ducking his head.

"I'm curious, Tommy." She released him. "Won't you at least give me a hint? If I'm going to do a good job working for the man, don't you think I ought to know a bit about him and his relationship to this community."

Tommy chewed his lower lip. "Okay," he said finally. "Before we got the chief, the law around here was pretty haphazard. Big guys with more muscle than sense. Wimps who let the cowboys whoop it up too much. My dad's the grocery store owner, and we used to get a lot of damage on Saturday nights if some of the Three Diamond boys decided to help themselves to a few free groceries. Even had one ride a horse through the aisles. Guess how much the Health Department liked that."

Deirdre grinned. The gangly youth might have a way of destroying proper grammer, but it was clear he was not stupid.

"Anyways . . ." Tommy went on, "when Chief Cassidy took the job, he cleaned things up in a hurry. No more trouble with the Diamond boys. He went out and had a talk with Old Man Salters who owns the place and that was the end of that. *And* he treats us kids like we're people. Doesn't push us around like one of the chiefs did. I like him." Respect was plain in his brown eyes.

"Thank you, Tommy." Deirdre hefted the bag of cleaning equipment. "I appreciate the information. I hope we can talk again soon." Tommy echoed the hope and said he would leave the cartons out back by the incinerator. Then he departed, leaving Deirdre wiser and happy to know where the incinerator was located. She had big plans for the instrument.

Sam patroled on foot, greeting townspeople with a smile and a touch to his Stetson. He remembered the first weeks of his tour here, how he had felt the distrust and downright suspicion of the locals. Wiseguy from California, they had seemed to be thinking. Playing at being a cowboy-cop. Then he had gradually unraveled the town's problems, settled matters with some of the larger ranchers regarding the behavior of their hands, and involved himself with the youth, thereby avoiding what seemed to be a traditional mistrust of authority by the adolescents. He knew of the nickname they'd laid on him, and it embarrassed him slightly. But he also had to admit that he liked it. After the way he'd been treated in L.A., it was a balm to his spirit to be, well . . . appreciated for the job he was doing.

This town and its people were his heart, he mused

as he walked the old wooden sidewalk of the one main street. It was as if he had always meant to be here, and the years in Los Angeles and the time he had spent in the Marines was just a bad dream. Oh, he had to admit that his childhood hadn't been bad until his dad had died one hot August morning tending the orange orchard that was their livelihood. He and his mom had tried, he remembered, but they had eventually been forced to sell out. Then they had moved into the city.

"Morning, Chief." The thin figure of John Edwards came out of the alley beside his supermarket. He was smiling broadly.

"Morning, John." Sam touched his Stetson. "Business okay?"

"Can't complain." John rubbed his hands on his butcher's apron. "Guess you can't none, either, from what young Tommy tells me." John's expression was a cross between mischief and shared male knowledge.

Sam took off his hat and smoothed his hair. "Can't say as I know what you're talking about, John," he confessed.

"The *lady*." John's expression was now definitely merrily conspiratorial. "Tommy told me about her. Matter of fact, can't hardly get the young'un to talk about anything else since he met her."

Sam resettled his hat. The breeze was starting to come up, so he set it firmly on his head. "Met her?" Suspicion rose. "How'd he do that, John?" he asked casually.

"Oh, all them cleaning supplies she ordered. You know, the ones she paid for in cash. And then she wanted cardboard boxes. Tommy hauled a bunch of 'em over to back of the station. Put 'em next to the incinerator. Said she asked him real polite how to use the thing. Oh, Sam, I tell you that boy's mighty taken with your lady. If he was about ten years older, I'd say you'd have a little competition on your hands.''

"John!" Sam felt a rising annoyance. "The lady's my secretary, nothing else. I just hired her this morning. Only *met* her this morning. And I'd appreciate it if you and Tommy wouldn't make any more of it than that.''

John grinned, obviously unconvinced of Sam's story. "Whatever you say, Chief," he said, chuckling and patting Sam on the shoulder. "You're the Law." Still chuckling and shaking his head, he went back into his store.

Sam continued his patrol, squinting his eyes against the dust raised by the strengthening breeze. It hadn't rained in a while, and the ground was too dry, he thought with part of his mind. Might make for some fire danger later on in the season.

The other part of his mind was on Deirdre Wilcox. Shoved down his throat by politics, was she going to upset the smooth system he had arranged in Lodge Pole? His local behavior had been completely celibate, a situation he had made by choice. No one here interested him, and when he felt the need of female companionship, he just took a few days leave and went to Denver where he knew a number of friendly women. He had never married, his life before his flight from the city had been too busy for him to give enough attention to a woman to keep her for long, and his image of himself was one of a lifelong bachelor. He could never adjust to another person demanding a partnership role in his life.

Now, according to John Edwards, the "Lady Wilcox" had taken it upon herself not only to disobey his orders to leave the cleaning to Mary's weekly visits, but apparently had given Tommy the impression that there was more between them than merely employment. His temper grew hotter.

But he continued his patrol. Let her have enough line to hang herself, he cautioned himself. If she had really messed the station up, he would have a perfect excuse to fire her, governor or no governor. Senator-daddy or no senator-daddy. She might be beautiful, have carloads of credentials, but if she turned out to be a disobedient spoiled brat, then she was going out on her pretty can! He shoved his hands into the pockets of his windbreaker and walked on.

Deirdre started with the bathroom, attacking the small place with vigor. She scrubbed the lime stains out of the sink and used disinfectant on all of the fixtures, and the tiled floor and walls as well. After some struggling, she forced the tiny window open, breathing the fresh smell of outdoor air as a relief from the pungent odors of the cleaning chemicals. The window, she noted, was barred on the outside. Since she had noted no toilet in the cell, she deduced that prisoners must be using this place, too. The window was too small for even someone her size to slip through, but it was clear that Chief Cassidy took no chances. The thought of being his prisoner gave her the shivers. With those icy eyes and massive frame, he could certainly be fearsome, she was sure.

But then, so could she. She remembered times when her willingness to argue and her logic had caused even her father to cave in on an issue. Not on this, however. In the end, she had been forced to admit that the physical evidence and her highly energetic life-style would probably shorten her life span by several decades if she didn't learn to move to the slower track. In many ways, she decided, she was grateful for the fact that Cassidy was such a slob. She could work all summer, contentedly, because there was so much to do!

As she wiped glass cleaner from the old, black-speckled mirror, she glanced at her own reflection and smiled. Quite a change from the way she had looked when she had arrived for the initial meeting with the man. Her carefully coiffured hair was still up in the sophisticated twist, but long tendrils had worked loose and now hung untidily around her face and shoulders. A smudge showed on her cheek from the lesson on using the incinerator she had taken from Tommy. The black mark accented one cheekbone. The latest fashion in makeup, she mused, making a face at herself.

She liked Tommy Edwards, she decided. And she was going to make him one of her projects this summer. The boy seemed to like her, too, and she hoped she could talk him into some grammar instruction. As she had thought at first, he had a quick mind, but the way he spoke disguised that. The boy would go nowhere in life, she knew, unless he learned better speech patterns. She was no English expert, but she could at least give him a start.

She swept the hall from the bathroom, past the cell, and out into the office. Tomorrow, she'd wear jeans and scrub the floor on her hands and knees to be sure she got every dust mote and slaughtered every lurking germ. No telling *what* some of Sam's prisoners had brought into the place on their shoes and clothing.

Wiping her hands on a paper towel, she then set to clearing off her desk chair. The coat was filthy, but she set it to one side. It could be washed and made marginally serviceable. Then she lifted the top papers, gasping in anger at what she discovered underneath.

Girlie magazines of all desciptions had been piled on *her* chair! Indignantly, she loaded the lot of them in the incinerator, watching with deep satisfaction as the pornography burned brightly with tongues of purple, blue, and red flames among the gold ones. In a *police* station, she fumed. Of all places. The calendar was going to go, too, she decided. But first, she would have to find a suitable substitute. The chief might want her to tolerate his officer, but if the man turned out to be a sexist dinosaur, he was going to find himself on her list of growing projects. A little enlightened education for that one on women as *persons*. Not sexual objects! She slammed the lid on the incinerator, enjoying the thrumming sound as the trash became literally trash.

Sam's stomach started to let him know that it was past noon just about the time he reached Sally Cantrell's café. He entered, taking off his hat and grinning as the café's owner greeted him heartily and with cheerful disrespect.

"Well, look what the cat's dragged in now," Sally said, pushing a stray lock of white hair back from her cheek. Her lined face was shiny with perspiration, and Sam saw that she was at her usual task of "slaving over a hot stove," cooking lunch for folks—working people who couldn't make it home for the meals, tourists, and ones like himself whom Sally labeled "too lazy to open a can of beans and eat it with a spoon." Their bantering relationship had begun shortly after his arrival and had grown to be almost legendary in the town. "Go get him, Sal," Sam heard Joe, the pharmacist at the drugstore, yell. Joe was eating a hamburger at the counter.

"Sally. Joe." Sam greeted everyone he knew by name. To the strangers, he gave a friendly nod. It never hurt to show tourists that the local law was friendly. As long as no rules were broken. "I had an urge to give myself an ulcer," he declared, turning his attention to Sally. "So I decided to eat your cooking for lunch, Mrs. Cantrell."

"Don't you go calling me that, Sam Cassidy!" Sally waved a spatula in his direction. Sam grinned. It always riled her to be called by her husband's name. He had run off and left her alone to manage the café years ago, and any mention of the rascal raised Sally's ire.

"I apologize," Sam said, his tone sincere. He slid into a seat at the counter, noting by the softened expression on her face that he was forgiven.

"What'll it be, Sam?" she asked, handing two

hamburger orders to her teenage granddaughter, a plump, bright-eyed girl who worked for her grandmother after school and during the summer tourist months. She gave Sam a shy smile and then scurried off with the plates. "If you're serious about the ulcer," Sally continued, "the chili's hotter than the blue hinges."

"No, Sal." Sam took his wallet out of his pocket. "I just need two cartons of milk and a couple of sandwiches to go. Got myself a new employee who I figure is getting pretty hungry by now."

"New officer?" Sally looked intrigued. Sam sighed inwardly. Once Sally found out about Deirdre, she'd have triple ammo to fire at him. The teasing would be unmerciful, and he steeled himself to bear it.

"New secretary," he explained. "The station's really a mess, and I thought—"

"Female?" Sally's faded blue eyes lit with interest. Sam nodded. Sally flipped a burger. "Young? Anyone I know?"

Sam doodled on the countertop with one finger. "Nobody you know, Sal. Woman from back East, out here for her health. Put mustard on my sandwich, please."

Sally started to assemble his order. "Woman, hmm," she said. "Wouldn't be that little gal took the senator's summer house, would it?" Knowing he couldn't weasel out of it or lie, Sam nodded. Sally whistled. "Sam, boy, I hear she is one fine-looking lady. She's working for *you*?"

"Sally, just make me the sandwiches."

She looked at him closely. "Already got to you, ain't she?" she whispered, mischief in her eyes. Her hands deftly wrapped the sandwiches in wax paper. Then she looked up, and Sam knew that she was about to make some public announcement designed to tease and embarrass him. He grabbed her arm gently.

"Leave it alone, Sal," he warned, staring directly into her eyes. "I'm not even sure she's going to last out the day."

Sally returned his gaze steadily. Then she nodded, giving him a genuine smile of friendship and understanding. Sam relaxed.

Deirdre was getting hungry, but she was determined to do one more thing before she set about satisfying that need. The office had grown stuffier by the minute, in spite of the fact that she had left the bathroom window and back door open. She wanted both the window that faced the street and the one that looked onto the alley wide open to help air the place out. The street-sided one came open with only a moderate amount of tugging. But the other one defied all her efforts. She broke several nails before she gave up and went in search of a toolbox. It would take at least a screwdriver and maybe a crowbar to get the thing up. Someone had apparently painted it shut.

She found a tool chest in the one closet and came up with a sturdy-looking screwdriver. Returning to the recalcitrant window, she struggled, tearing more nails and snagging the left knee of her panty hose, but finally, with an anguished screech, the obstinate sash flew upward. A gust of warm air rushed in, and Deirdre turned to see that her action had caused a major disaster. The breeze that blew in drew energy from the air coming in the other openings, and the loose papers on the chief's desk began to execute a slow pirouette. She hastened to collect them before everything ended up on the floor, but the front door opened suddenly and the breeze became a tornado. She scrambled in vain for the papers.

"What in *hell* is going on here!" Chief Sam Cassidy's voice boomed in the small room, and Deirdre found herself wishing fervently that she could crawl underneath the swirling papers and hide forever!

THREE

Sam slammed the door, not sure whether to keep on yelling or to burst into laughter at the sight. She stood, papers flying all around her—one sheet of carbon settled on her messed-up hairdo like an odd cap, looking like a guilty child. All of the sophisticated veneer was gone. Her stocking was torn, a streak of dirt smudged her cheek, her blouse had come partially out of her waistband. In short, Miss Deirdre Wilcox had been reduced to a disaster herself—one as complete as she had earlier claimed his office was. He pushed back the brim of his hat and surveyed the confusion.

"I just wanted to let in a little fresh air." Deirdre seemed to have regained her composure. She reached up and brushed the carbon paper off her hair. "Guess I overdid it a bit." She gave him a sheepish smile.

Sam decided not to let her off too easily. In order to have opened the window he had deliberately painted shut, she must have had to go to considerable trouble. She certainly had the appearance of a woman who had been hard at work. He looked at her closely, noting that the perfectly manicured hands were now dirty and sporting broken nails. He tossed the bag containing lunch on the now-empty desk.

"Isn't 'overdoing' the reason why you're exiled out here, Miss Workaholic?" he asked, keeping his tone angry. "What are you trying to do? Have a heart attack on *my* time? That'll certainly earn me points with my bosses!"

"I just—"

"You just sit down!" he roared, pointing to the chair in front of his desk. She obeyed, looking at the littered floor and biting her lower lip. Her damaged hands curled in her lap like hurt animals.

Sam took off his hat and hung up his windbreaker. He shut the back door, noting that smoke issued from the incinerator. What, he wondered, had she consigned to the blaze. She had promised not to touch anything related to official business. A quick glance showed him that Andy's beloved calendar was still on the wall. He sat down at his desk, regarding her as he would a prisoner he was about to interrogate.

But she was no longer staring guiltily at the floor. Her blue eyes were on his in a direct gaze—with no apology in their depths whatsoever.

"If," she said in a steady tone, "you had kept things filed and covered, this would never have happened."

"*If*," he countered, "you hadn't tried to get months of work done in one morning, it wouldn't have happened. I should have nailed that window shut. Then maybe I could have gotten back in time to stop you.''

"I was going to look for a crowbar next." Her chin lifted. "It gets far too stuffy in here. But I don't suppose you notice since you're out on the street where the air is fresh."

"Where the air is *windy*. I told you that it picks up in the afternoons. But that's not the issue, Miss Wilcox." He slammed a hand down on the desk. "The issue is your behavior!"

Deirdre jumped involuntarily at the sound of his palm slapping the desk. It sounded like a gunshot or a whiplash. But she refused to be intimidated. She recognized bullying when she saw it! "I admit to keeping busy this morning," she said calmly. "But all I did was clean the bathroom, sweep the hall, and get rid of . . . certain unnecessary paper. I was preparing to start on the office, but wanted some fresh air. That's all."

"I told you cleaning wasn't your job." His eyes were stormy. "I have a cleaning woman—"

"Who isn't worth a dime." Deirdre rose. "Follow me," she said, beckoning in a challenging fashion.

Unwillingly, and sensing that she had once more wrested control of the situation from his hands, Sam followed. When they reached the bathroom, she made a broad gesture, inviting him to look inside. Her face wore a smug expression.

But when he obeyed, amazement filled him. The room was absolutely spotless. Probably cleaner than it had been when the place was first built. Somehow, she had managed to restore a shine to the fixtures, and his reflection in the old, spotted mirror was clearer than he could ever remember. Round one to the little lady.

"It does look better," he conceded, noting that even the end of the toilet paper had been folded into a neat point. If Andy saw it like that, he'd die laughing, but Sam had been in hotels where it was a touch of elegance applied automatically.

"Better?" She stepped in the room beside him. "I would have had to autoclave the place to get it any cleaner. You could eat off the floor." She glared up at him defiantly.

Sam looked down at her, suddenly aware of her presence as a woman. The bathroom didn't give them much space, and if he moved a millimeter, his chest would touch her breasts. Breasts that filled the silky blouse in an inviting way, especially now that the blouse was half out of the skirt. He felt his pulses start to beat faster.

"I don't think we need to do that," he said softly. "But you have done a fine job, Deirdre. You made a mistake in opening the window, but everyone's entitled to a few of those. Lord knows, I've made my share." He reached up and tucked a strand of hair back behind her ear, unable to resist the urge to touch her. "I'll bet you're hungry. Let's go have lunch."

She hesitated, not quite understanding his sudden shift from anger to almost tenderness. "You . . . you aren't angry with me?" she asked.

Sam smiled. "Only at your working too hard. As for the mess in the office, I guess I deserve that one. I never could learn to deal with paperwork. Hate it and keep putting it off. Maybe this is a warning to get my act together and take organization and filing seriously for a change.'' He put his hand on her shoulder and gave her a gentle push toward the door. "Come on, Super Secretary. Luncheon awaits."

She obeyed, feeling the warmth of his big hand through the thin silk fabric of the blouse. "You're right," she confessed as they walked side by side down the short hallway. "I plunged into this just like I have everything else—full speed ahead. I guess a change of locale doesn't change the person inside."

"It can help." His tone was kind. "If you're willing to work on yourself for that change."

"Voice of experience?"

He nodded, but said nothing else. He sat and opened the sack he had brought in and handed her a carton of milk and a sandwich. So much for details about Chief Mysterious's past, she thought. But then he surprised her by asking a personal question.

"You don't have to answer," he said, unwrapping his sandwich. "But I'm kind of curious. You're young, obviously strong." He eyed the window. "Why were your doctor and father so worried about you that they went to so much trouble to get you away from Washington? Why not just talk sense into you and get you to give up a few projects?"

Deirdre hesitated. She was reluctant to talk about it, but maybe if she opened up, he would reciprocate. She knew she had no logical reason for giving a darn about him, but that niggle of interest was there, like an itch. He *intrigued* her. So she began to talk.

"It's hereditary," she explained. "Both my mother and my grandmother died young of heart attacks. It's rare in women, but my line seems to carry it. Ever since Mom died when I was twelve, Daddy's had me in for a complete checkup every year. There've been great improvements in diagnosis and medication, but when I seemed unable to stop myself from working a killing pace, my father decided banishment was the only solution.''

Sam smiled wryly. "He was wrong. He'd have a fit if he saw what you've done during the morning.''

Deirdre pushed loose hair back from her face. "I *will* slow down. I was just so excited at the new challenge that I fell back into old habits. I swear I'll waltz through the afternoon in a slow dance.''

"Don't promise me, Deirdre. Promise yourself.'' His voice and expression were stern, but there was a light of warmth in his eyes. Those *eyes,* she thought. If you caught them just right, you could see the inner man. He was a good actor—she recognized the techniques from other law-enforcement people she had known and from politicians, both male and female. It was a talent that came with the territory. But if you studied a person long enough, you could learn to read them behind the facade. Suddenly, she decided to open up a bit more,

"There was another reason I finally agreed, however reluctantly, to leave Washington,'' she said softly.

"What was that?'' Sam tilted his head back and drained his milk, and she watched the strong muscles of his neck work as he swallowed.

"There was a man . . .'' she began.

The milk suddenly went down the wrong way, and Sam started to choke and sputter. He held up his hand, indicating to her that he was okay, but it took a few seconds of coughing before he could speak. "I always do that when I drink out of a carton," he lied. Her confession of a serious relationship had caught him by surprise, although he wondered why. Surely a woman as beautiful as she was had suitors by the dozens. Why should he be surprised that she had a special beau? He narrowed his eyes.

It was because she had an unattached *feel* about her, he decided, After years of field-playing, he could usually sense when a woman had a man of her own and when she was open to his casual advances. Deirdre somehow didn't seem to fit any category. That must have been what surprised him so much.

"I said there *was* a man," she explained, not seeming to notice his scrutiny. Her features grew sad. "He appeared to be everything wonderful wrapped up in one gorgeous package. We were about to be engaged."

Sam held his breath. Who had dumped whom? For some reason it seemed important to him.

"I was all starry-eyed," she went on. "Then gradually it began to dawn on me. He was using our relationship to further his own career. He was perfect, never picking a fight, even when I *knew* he disagreed with me. That was abnormal. People in love can fight. Ought to when they have a difference of opinion."

"But there was more."

"He wanted introductions. We would go to parties, and he would ever so sweetly urge me to help him meet this person or that one. Always someone who could be an aid to him. He cleverly never actually ignored me, but after a time I began to wise up. And when we were talking, I started to realize that he wasn't listening unless I was talking politics. Then it was as if the bastard was taking notes!''

Sam found himself slightly shocked by her language and anger. She had even more spirit than he thought. No doubt in his mind who did the dumping, and he felt a surge of relief at the knowledge. For some reason, the idea of her carrying a torch for an old flame bothered him.

"So what did you do?" he asked encouragingly.

Her azure eyes developed a wicked gleam. "I watched and waited," she said. "Then when he took me out for a romantic evening and presented me with an engagement ring, I very calmly explained that I had figured him out, and that he could take the ring and—"

"I get the picture." Sam chuckled and raised his hands. "Remind me never to get you riled, lady."

"Oh, there's more." She was wide-eyed innocence personified, but he knew that what he was about to hear would be a far from innocent story.

"Go on," he encouraged. The more he knew about this woman the better, he decided. The safety of the citizens of his town could someday depend on her.

"He wouldn't give up. Denied his motivations and declared that he did love me. He would not admit his opportunistic spirit." Her eyes flashed sapphire. "Right in the middle of a very elegant, very full-of-important-people restaurant, he started to manhandle me. He tried to shove the ring on my finger. That's when I did it."

"Did what?" Sam found that he was sitting on the edge of his chair.

"Punched him out," the mussed but ladylike

woman across from him declared. "Cold-cocked the son-of-a-bitch with a wine bottle I grabbed from a nearby table. I caught him right in the chin, and he went down for the count. Then I took the ring . . ."

"You didn't!"

Deirdre started to laugh, and Sam decided he liked the sound of it. Low and soft, it was pleasing to his ears. "I didn't do what you're thinking," she said. "I just tossed it into a fountain on the way out of the restaurant. I heard that when he came to, the ring was all he asked about. He went in after it, shoes, socks, and all. I never heard from him again."

"I can't imagine why." Sam leaned back and studied her. What a contradictory person she was. This morning, he wouldn't have given two cents for her company. Now, he was thoroughly enjoying himself, and it wasn't just because she was good to look at. She might have lived it too hard, but it was clear to him that her life had been interesting, and he wondered how she was going to cope with the occasional tedium of small-town life. Would it put *more* stress on her to fight boredom? He made a mental note to offer to take her into Jackson Hole for a checkup by his doctor sometime. There was a small clinic in Lodge Pole run by a paramedic, but Sam still had reservations about the man's ability to handle much more than first-aid situations. Deirdre would need a diagnostician, and George Bennett was one of the best Sam had known.

She chatted on while they ate, giving him interesting details of her experiences as a senator's daughter. She loved her father, that was plain to see whenever she spoke of him. Her expression softened, and she always smiled. Sam decided that it must have been a tremendous wrench for both of them for her to come out here. But the fact that her father had insisted proved to Sam that he put his daughter's well-being above any other consideration. He decided he would like to meet the parent of this extraordinary woman.

"Well . . ." she sid finally, wrapping up her wax paper and depositing it neatly into the trash can. "That's enough about me. Now it's your turn. Tell me about Sam Cassidy."

He rolled his wrapper into a ball and tossed it at the can. It missed. Deirdre watched as a cold veil dimmed the light in his eyes, and she realized with disappointment that she was going to get nothing. No trade-off for her self-revelation.

"Not much to tell," he said, rising and going over to pick up the wrapper. Before he tossed it away, he tore it into little pieces. "I grew up near Los Angeles, was a Marine, became a cop, went to night school to get my degrees, then I left to come here."

Oh, no you don't, she thought. "With all that educational investment, you just chucked a career in a big city department and came out to live in the middle of *nowhere*?"

Sam reached for his hat and coat. "Like you, I did it for my health." He gestured at the room. "I'd appreciate it if this was in some kind of order before Andy takes over. He's not much better than I am, but it would kind of startle him to find the office on the floor." He opened the front door.

"Speaking of Andy . . ." Deirdre began, planning to tell him of the destroyed magazines. But the door closed abruptly.

Damn him, she thought, hitting the desk with her fist. She wasn't asking for every intimate detail of his life. Just a little friendly exchange. Was that too much to ask?

Muttering to herself about clam-mouthed police chiefs, she made her way down the hall to the bathroom. Using the antique mirror, she cleaned her face and carefully reapplied light makeup. Then she tried to rewind her hair, but gave up since she couldn't find enough pins to keep it tight. Instead, she combed it out, letting the wavy mane fall over her shoulders and down her back. Try to understand men, she thought. She had thought that Sam was working up to being friendly, but evidently he still resented her and had no intention of opening up to her. She shook her hair back and regarded herself.

Maybe he had something shameful in his past, she decided. Something he would be ashamed to share with a stranger. That made her feel warmer toward him, but it also raised doubts. If he had done something wrong, were people like Tommy Edwards right to put so much trust in him? Would he fail if a real crisis came along. Something he couldn't solve with that impressive body and massive hands?

Well, enough speculation, she told herself. Time to get to work. And there was certainly plenty of it.

She retrieved several boxes from the back alley and started to pick up the papers, not trying to divide or file them in any order yet. Just get them off the floor for starters. She was getting a rhythm to it, when the phone rang, startling her.

"Lodge Pole Police Station," she said into the receiver. "May I help you?"

"Where's the chief?" The voice was old-sounding and querulous. "I want to talk to him!"

"I'll relay any message," Deirdre said in her most professionally soothing tone. "Now just tell me what the problem is, and I'll have Chief Cassidy on it right away."

"Who're you?" Angry now.

"I'm the chief's new secretary. Please just give me—"

"Got him a secretary now, eh?" The voice sounded suddenly amused. "Are you pretty, missy? Chief oughta have a lady friend. Ain't right a man like him—"

"Excuse me," Deirdre interrupted as politely as she could, keeping her temper by only a short thread. "But this is an official phone, and I'm not permitted to discuss personal matters over it. Could you please just give me the details of your problem."

"All right, missy." The angry tone was back. "Tell him that some cussed dog's been digging in my garden again. Tell him if he don't enforce the leash laws, I'm going to start taking my shotgun to every one of 'em I see." The caller hung up abruptly.

Deirdre stared at the receiver. No name, few details. How was she to call the chief on this one?

She sighed and hung up. Many times when she had worked for her father she had had to deal with strange phone calls, but this one took the cake. She could guess that the caller was elderly and bad-tempered. And that he or she had a garden. Beyond that . . .

She went over to the dispatch machine and depressed the button. "One," she said into the microphone.

Sam answered almost immediately, his deep voice carrying well over the old instrument. She told him what had happened and heard him chuckle. "Don't worry," he reassured her. "I know the party. I'll take care of it." Then his voice was gone.

Deirdre turned back to her task. It was his town, all right, if he could decipher the identity of the caller from the information she'd given him. She was stacking a pile of the scattered papers when the door burst open. A tall, handsome blond man stood framed there for a moment, astonishment on his face. He looked at the littered office, and then his gaze settled on her.

"Oh, my God," he whispered. "I've died and gone to heaven." He closed the door with an almost reverent move, never taking his eyes off of her. "You can't possibly be the senator's bra—daughter we're saddled . . . getting for a secretary?"

"Andy Davis?" Deirdre asked, keeping her tone cool.

"At your every command!" He swept off the cowboy hat he wore and bowed low. "I expected a pale, overweight city woman. *You* are a goddess!"

"Officer Davis. I burned your pornography. If you want to keep your calendar, I suggest you take it home. It's entirely unfitting for a police station."

His expression changed from one of delight to one of horror. "Burned my magazines?" he cried. "*All* of them?"

Deirdre nodded.

FOUR

Sam drove the Jeep Wagoneer up the gravel-paved back streets of Lodge Pole until he reached Agatha Jaspers's small house. Cabin really, he thought, as he got out of the heavy-duty vehicle. Aggie's husband had been a small-time rancher whose death had left his wife some real estate and a meager life-insurance policy, he had learned from local gossip. She had sold the land and moved into town, where she didn't do much but exist and complain. But this was the third time this week her garden had been vandalized, and he knew she depended on the vegetables to help her through the winter. Unlikable or not, Agatha was one of the people he had sworn to protect, and he intended to do it.

She greeted him at the door with a tirade he barely heard. He took off his hat and asked gently where the damage was this time. Still fussing, Agatha led him to the backyard. He followed, thinking that the old woman couldn't be more than ninety pounds, dripping wet. Anyone or anything that deprived her of food deserved punishment.

"There," she said, pointing to a section of high fence that been downed. The garden wasn't totally destroyed, but it would take a lot of work to get it back in order. "Cussed dogs went and knocked the fence clean over," Agatha complained.

Sam resettled his hat and walked over to the place of forced entry. The wood was splintered and cracked, and he doubted it was the work of any carnivore. Several other homes in town had had flower gardens dug up, and that he had put down to loose pets, but this. . . .

"Mrs. Jaspers," he said, turning to the tiny, angry woman. "I'll send someone over to fix this fence . . ."

"Ain't taking no charity!"

Sam sighed. Coming from a world where welfare had reached the point of a tidal wave, the pioneer stubbornness of some of Lodge Pole's residents still amazed him. "It isn't charity if I think you've been victimized in some way and I send my officer to repair the damage to the fence," he said patiently. "He won't fix your garden. I'm afraid you'll have to do that yourself."

"Well, all right." She crossed her arms over her thin chest. "You thinking it's a human doing this?" She regarded him with suspicion, as if she thought he himself might be the perpetrator.

Sam tilted his hat back on his head. "Could be. Why don't you go on back inside out of the wind, Mrs. Jaspers. Let me take a look around and see what I can find."

She hesitated, then gave him a curt nod. "All right, Chief," she said. Then she surprised him by giving him an impish grin. "Give my regards to your new lady friend," she added. "Sounds mighty pretty over the phone."

Sam groaned inwardly as he watched the old woman leave the garden. In addition to being a complainer, she was also known as a gossip. He was going to have to come down hard on any rumors that he and Deirdre were involved. But, he thought as he bent to his task of examining the scene, any fool would know to expect them with him being single and her being so . . .

Well, Cassidy, he asked himself. Her being so *what*? He gently moved some soil with his hand, studying a mark in the dirt. Deirdre Wilcox being so pretty—no, beautiful—and then so willing—overly willing—to work like a trooper? He had seen plenty of nice-looking women working in the Department back in L.A., but rarely had he known one willing to clean toilets, break carefully cultivated nails on window sashes, as well as cheerfully accepting the task of filing an office floor full of years of accumulated papers. And then there had been her willingness to tell him, a stranger, about her past. Even he didn't have the guts to do that. Of course, he reflected as he moved around the ruined garden, he had more reason to keep quiet than she did. The light he saw occasionally in her eyes during lunch wouldn't have been there very long if he had opened up the way she had. Sam took out a notebook and started to make some sketches of the scene.

*   *   *

Deirdre planted her feet firmly, crossed her arms over her chest, and glared at Andy Davis. His tanned face had reddened considerably, and his string of complaints sounded like that of a small child deprived of a favorite toy.

"Some of those were *collector's* items, dammit— 'scuze me, Miss Wilcox," he said. He stared at the empty chair as if he couldn't believe his magazines were really gone.

"Did the chief know they were under those other papers?" she asked, using an accusing tone.

"Well . . ." Andy spread out his hands. "I don't exactly know. I mean, you know the way he keeps records." He grinned winningly and gestured around the office. "Doesn't look as if things have improved much."

"There was an accident," she replied coldly. "Now, if you'd please pitch in, I think we can have this all picked up in a few minutes." To her surprise, he obeyed her request.

"Haven't seen you around before," he commented conversationally, and instinctively Deirdre realized that the paper dolls had been dismissed in favor of the real thing. "All I know about you is that the chief was purely furious when he got that letter from the governor . . ."

"Please." Deirdre held up a hand. "I got enough of that from him this morning. I agree that political favor-calling isn't the best way to do business, but my father insisted. And I doubt I would have gotten the job if he hadn't. Your chief doesn't seem particularly fond of the idea of having office help."

Andy grinned. "He does like to do things his own

way,'' he agreed. ''I think that's why he moved out here. Got pushed around by the system in California and didn't like it. Here, as long as the town's happy, he's pretty much free to handle things the way he likes.''

''So I can see.'' Deirdre stacked another pile of papers. ''With another man, that could be a problem, but I get the impression that Chief Cassidy is well thought of.''

''Honey . . .'' Andy said seriously. ''There ain't a man in this town who wouldn't follow him into . . . Well, you get my meaning.''

Deirdre pondered the information. She longed to know more but didn't want to seem a gossip or a busybody. Bending to her task, she noted that Andy Davis had moved closer.

''I was just a rookie,'' he said. ''Graduated from the Law Enforcement Academy down in Douglas, came back here to home to visit, and Sam he recruited me on the spot.'' Deirdre detected the same hero worship she had seen in Tommy's eyes.

''I wouldn't think a young man would find much of a future here,'' she said, thinking of the youthful movers and shakers she had known in Washington. ''I'd think a larger town or city would provide more opportunity for advancement.''

''Advancement?'' Andy laughed. ''Honey, I just want to have a decent job, which I got, and find me a pretty little gal to settle down with and raise a family. What're you doing Saturday night?''

Her sharp retort to the abrupt invitation was cut short by Sam Cassidy bursting into the office like an express train. He didn't bother to shut the door behind him or to greet either one of them. He just hurried to the gun cabinet and took out an odd-looking rifle. His rugged, tanned features were set with tension.

"What is it, Chief?" Andy hurried to his side, reaching for a conventional shotgun. Deirdre stood frozen, unable to comprehend the sudden action.

"Big moose making mincemeat of the north end of town," Sam muttered, checking his rifle. "Got to put him out of commission before he hurts somebody. Already wrecked some backyards."

Deirdre finally found her voice. "You aren't going to *shoot* someone just because they caused some vandalism?" she asked, horrified. Sam Cassidy might have his way around the town, but she was not going to let him get away with what could amount to murder! She moved to block the doorway, shutting it and placing herself in the path of anyone who would try to pass her.

Sam settled his hat and glared at her. "I've never killed anyone in my life, Miss Wilcox," he said, his voice chill. "I don't intend to start now." She could see strange emotions in his green eyes, but the firm set of his mouth almost convinced her.

"But the guns . . ." she began.

He raised his eyes. "There's a real *moose* out there," he said. "No drunken cowboy. This is a tranquilizer rifle. Andy's shotgun is just for backup." He moved toward her, his large frame and angry expression almost making her quail. "Now get out of the way!" he said. "Property and maybe lives are in danger." Deirdre moved with as much dignity as she could muster. Sam touched his hat and said thanks in a sarcastic tone. Then he was out of the door.

Andy's blue eyes held laughter as he followed his chief. He glanced at her. "Don't ever question the boss, honey," he whispered. "Come on out. Watch the show."

Deirdre felt a little dizzy. What a strange world she had been dropped into. Dangerous animals instead of men in the streets. For a moment, disorientation made the room swim, then she gathered her sense of reality and followed the two lawmen out into the blustery, sunny afternoon.

But the scene that met her eyes was so surreal that she had to grab at the doorjamb to keep her equilibrium. It was both absurd and frightening at the same time. Sam stood in the middle of the street, looking for all the world like the hero of a western movie preparing for a shootout with the bad guy. His long legs were spread in a sturdy stance, and the butt of his rifle was rammed against his shoulder as he sighted carefully along the barrel. The streets were lined with curious onlookers, but they wore modern dress instead of pioneer garb. And the villain whom Sam was facing down was hardly the typical squinty-eyed rogue of the western-genre films.

Deirdre stared. It was a real moose. A huge animal that seemed to her to be almost ten feet tall. Mean little eyes gleamed ruby-brown underneath wide, spatulate antlers. Antlers, she realized, could crush in a man's rib cage before the gigantic hooves mashed the rest of him. She felt a sudden rush of terror for Sam's safety and was unable to let a gasp escape her lips.

Andy turned and looked at her, an odd expression on his face. He held the shotgun at ready but didn't seem too concerned. "He'll be fine," he whispered.

But to Deirdre, it didn't look as if Sam Cassidy was going to be fine at all. He seemed to be deliberately provoking the enormous animal by yelling at it, calling it names that would have been funny under any other circumstances. The animal had seemed to be wondering which direction to take, but Sam's figure and voice drew its attention. The huge head lowered, the nostrils in the long Roman nose flared, and one hoof scraped repeatedly at the street.

"Come on, you," Sam yelled, releasing his grip on the rifle for a second to sweep off his hat and throw it midway between himself and the moose. Another scrape of the hoof, and Deirdre watched Sam resettle his aim.

But just when it seemed as if the moose was going to take the bait, a small child in the assembled onlookers made a cry. The big head swiveled in the direction of the boy. Deirdre's heart almost stopped, but her body didn't. As if galvanized by a spirit she didn't know she possessed, she ran into the street behind Sam and let out the wildest rebel yell she could muster. The horned head aimed at her, and she heard the popping sound of the rifle as Sam fired.

The moose let out a bellow and charged. But it stopped to gore the hat. Snorting with fury, it took out its obvious rage on the Stetson. Deirdre watched, frozen again and unable to move. Then a strong arm lifted her as if she were made of feathers and threw her onto the sidewalk behind Andy. When she recovered her feet, she saw that Sam was still standing in the street, facing down the moose who had clearly finished with the hat and was ready for larger game.

It lurched forward, staggering as the drug seemed to be taking effect. The sound of its hooves echoed in the street. Sam drew his revolver, but stood like a rock. The moose snorted and took another step forward. Deirdre saw Andy raise the shotgun.

"Don't shoot," she heard Sam say quietly as the monster advanced unsteadily on him. "I gave him enough to take down an elephant, Andy."

"Does *he* know that?" Andy didn't lower the shotgun.

Deirdre looked from one man to the other, thinking that they were both crazy. Sam should at least be running, hoping that the drug would take effect before the beast could catch him and do to him what it had done to his hat. But her own actions had been so uncharacteristically brave that she was still stunned so she could only watch as events unfolded.

The moose lurched once more, bellowing weakly but furiously. Then it collapsed, just a few feet from Sam's dusty boots. A cheer went up from the audience. Deirdre watched Sam holster his gun and heard him give a sigh of relief. "Down for the count," he muttered.

"I'll call Game and Fish," Andy said, lowering and then breaking the shotgun.

"Get 'em to ship him all the way over the pass," Sam said, studying the moose. "He's not afraid of people anymore, and he'll be a danger to any settlement or campground." He strode around the snoring animal and picked his battered hat off the street. He looked at it for a long moment, then turned to glare at the small figure of Deirdre Wilcox.

She still stood in the same spot where he had thrown her, and she looked as if she had been shot with a little of the same stuff he'd used on the moose. Emotions mixed furiously in him. What she had done had probably averted a disaster, but it had put her in terrible danger. If he hadn't gotten that round off. . . . If, for some reason, the rifle had jammed, the moose would have charged over him to get to her. That ungodly shriek had attracted more of the animal's attention than any of his vocalizations. Any number of conditions could have him staring down at the mangled and battered figure of the woman instead of his hat. His strongest emotion suddenly became anger.

"You!" he shouted, pointing at her. "You were put in *my* care, and you nearly got yourself killed!" A murmur from the crowd behind him bothered him, but he strode over to where she stood without looking back. Her big blue eyes stared at him as if he were some fearsome demon.

"Miss Wilcox," he said, making his tone as intimidating and cold as possible. "I will not accept responsibility for a woman who obviously cares nothing for her own safety. As of this moment, you're fired, and I don't care if your daddy gets the *president* on my butt." He brushed past her and entered the station.

Deirdre felt the shock, terror, and amazement slowly drain out of her until there was nothing left but cold, icy anger. How *dare* he! She had distracted the moose with her yell, otherwise things might have gone much worse. And for him to stand there like John Wayne, waiting for the animal to tromp him rather than give an inch. . . . Well, that showed a macho stupidity that she wasn't impressed by one iota. Fired! Like *hell* she was!

Her eyes focused on the crowd along the street. They were still waiting, breathless, as if they knew another scene was to be played out for their entertainment. Resentment for their attitude rushed through her. If the child had been properly indoors where he should have been, considering the danger, none of this would have had to happen. Sam would have had a clear shot at the moose, and she wouldn't have had to make a fool of herself by using the yell she'd learned as a child in Atlanta. She dusted off her skirt where the sidewalk had dirtied it when Sam, idiotically thinking she couldn't take care of herself, had dumped her. "I believe this little spectacle is over," she said loudly and sternly. "You all might as well go inside and be about your own business." Then she turned and stalked into the station.

Andy was on the phone, but his eyes opened wide at her entrance. Sam's scowl deepened.

"I meant what I said, Miss Wilcox," he said, laying the tranquilizing rifle on the desk. "I won't have anyone working for me who's into personal heroics."

"Maybe she just wanted to accept the date I offered her for Saturday night," Andy interrupted, his hand over the telephone receiver and a leer on his handsome face.

Sam felt like someone had hit him in the stomach. A date with Andy? Deirdre couldn't possibly be considering going out with the county's most notorious lothario. But how could he warn her?

"Officer Davis . . ." she said, her southern accent breaking into the cultured tones she had acquired in Washington. "Much as I am flattered by your invitation, I don't make it a habit of being escorted by men who have to get their kicks reading pornography."

Sam felt himself relax a bit. She wasn't taking Andy up on it. But how could she know that his officer had a weakness for photographed female flesh as well as the real thing? The calendar was hardly an indication of Andy's reading habits.

"Chief Cassidy," she said to him. "I took the liberty of burning about six or seven dozen magazines that were hidden under some papers on what *used* to be my chair. The material they contained was hardly germane to police work, and I believe that you had given me permission to destroy anything I found that didn't directly relate."

Sam nodded, wondering what all this formal talk was leading up to. He had fired her and had made it clear why. The fear he had experienced for her earlier returned. She was a self-destructive person, and he suddenly found himself hoping she would stay around and allow him to become her friend. Let him see if he could help her.

"I wasn't aware of Andy's using police time to indulge his tastes in literature," he said, trying to smile at her, but failing under her icy azure glare. "You did the right thing."

"I also intend to leave the cleaning supplies here that I bought for your use," she continued, gathering up her purse and jacket. "I strongly suggest that you find a cleaning person with a bit more attention to detail. That cell is a disgrace, as was the bathroom, and you could find yourself up on civil-rights charges if someone were to get ill from germs in there."

"Oh, really." Sam took in her defiant pose. "Do you have any suggestions as to a possible candidate?"

"Frankly, I could care less what you do with this place once I walk out that door." She lifted her chin. "It's clear to me that not one of you people have a grain of common sense. Those people lining the street to watch you face that innocent animal! It was ludicrous. A parody of *High Noon*. Although in the movie, I had no difficulty telling the hero from the villain." She hefted her purse onto one shoulder and slung her jacket over her back by her hooked fingers.

Sam was speechless. She was giving him a verbal dressing-down he in no way deserved. It had been *her* doing that had caused a simple police action to dissolve into a possible disaster.

"One more thing, Chief," she said. He was too angry to answer, so he just cocked his head to one side, staring at her. "I'm not fired," she shot at him. "I *quit*." Sam watched mutely as she turned and marched out of the door, slamming it behind her.

For a long, long moment, silence filled the station. Then: "Chief . . ." Andy asked. "What's 'germane' mean?"

FIVE

Deirdre stalked down the street, noting with satisfaction that no one was out of doors. The wind whipped her hair and chilled her through her silk blouse but she wasn't about to stop and put on her coat. Anyway, the cold breeze matched her mood.

Someone had hauled the moose to one side of the road, and the only sign of life in the big animal was the regular rise and fall of its belly as it breathed. Ugly, she thought. Just like this place. She wanted to go home.

But her own good sense cautioned her against overreacting. She had come here to rest, and rest she would. She would learn to take life one day at a time, *and* she would learn never to try to help green-eyed cops again. They were clearly too thick-headed to understand her actions.

She was passing a small café when a white-haired, large-bosomed woman came boiling out of the building. "There you are, you wonderful girl," the woman cried, throwing her arms around Deirdre. "You and Sam! You saved my grandson!"

Deirdre pulled back, intending to scold the woman for letting the boy out in the first place, but her tear-filled eyes and wide grin made Deirdre realize how rude that would be.

"I just acted out of instinct," she confessed. "When I think about it, I get the shivers." She smiled weakly and hugged herself.

"Well, me, too." The big woman released her, but kept a large arm draped over Deirdre's shoulders. "Tell you what, missy. The café's quiet right now, and my granddaughter can handle things. What's say you let me buy you a drink. Least I can do."

"A drink?" Deirdre frowned. There were no lounges where two women could go in Lodge Pole, only saloons that looked like last-century male bastions.

"Sure. I couldn't hear all Cassidy said to you, but I figure you two had a bit of a row after the dust settled. Bet you could use some calming down." The woman steered her in the direction of the nearest saloon. A Miller sign flashed in the dusty window. "I'm Sally Cantrell," she added. "I run the café."

Reluctantly, but feeling she had little choice without making a fuss, Deirdre allowed herself to be led into the dim, smoky interior of the bar. The older woman was greeted warmly by the few occupants.

"Hey, Sally," the lean bartender called. "What's your pleasure? You and the little heroine?"

Deirdre squared her shoulders. "My name's Deirdre Wilcox, and I'd like a double vodka martini, please.''

"Usual for me, Charlie," Sally Cantrell said. She propelled Deirdre to a booth. "Better get used to being called a heroine, Dee," she said, taking up much of the seat across the small table from Deirdre. "Folks appreciate what you done out there almost as much as I do. If that moose had headed into the crowd . . .''

"You shouldn't have been . . . gawking," Deirdre said gently, trying to slip a little local language into her speech and at the same time letting Sally know how she felt.

But the older woman just laughed. "Most excitement we've had around here since Cassidy faced down some motorcycle boys last month." She grinned. "Something happens on the street here, and everybody comes out to watch. It's just natural."

Deirdre thought of the contrast with the city, where at the slightest sign of trouble, every living soul who wasn't directly involved headed for the nearest bolt hole. This *was* another world. But now her curiosity was aroused. "What did he do with the riders?" she asked, unable to resist the question, even though she was simmering with resentment at the big policeman.

The bartender delivered their drinks, and Sally knocked her jigger of what appeared to be bourbon back quickly. "Oh," she said, chuckling. "They was sitting outside the bar down the street, making dirty remarks to the women, scaring the kids, and drinking beer out in the open. Mean-looking bastards. Andy backed Cassidy up, and the two of them ambled down the street and discussed travel arrangements with the scum.''

"Travel arrangements?'' Deirdre took a sip of her martini. It had too much vermouth, but the warmth made her muscles start to relax.

Sally grinned. "As I hear tell, Sam suggested that unless they pull out of Lodge Pole right away, when they did go, they might just run across a little piano wire strung across the road somewhere down the line.''

"Could he *do* that?'' Deirdre took a long sip.

Sally shrugged. "Didn't need to. You know what he's like. Them bums lit out of here like their tails was on fire. Word must of gotten around, too, 'cause we ain't had any others come through this spring.''

Deirdre listened silently while Sally detailed other times that Sam Cassidy had used his wits instead of his position and strength to enforce the law and keep peace. It was too bad, she decided after a while, that they had parted under such angry circumstances. Her earlier impression that Sam was a man worth getting to know was only reinforced by Sally's recital.

"So . . .'' the older woman said at last. "You're going to be working for him. You'll have plenty of chances to see what I've been talking about.''

Deirdre drained her drink. "No,'' she said, "I won't. He fired me, then I quit.''

"What?'' Sally's face registered amazement. "After what you done this afternoon. Why, I'll . . . !''

Deirdre put a hand on the other woman's arm. "Don't do anything, Sally. Sam and I are just too different to ever get along anyway.'' She hesitated. "If you want to do me any favors, let me know if there's a part-time job or something that doesn't require much mental work or effort." She detailed the reasons for her being in Lodge Pole. "I need the rest, but I can't just do *nothing*," she added.

Sally got a glint in her eyes. "Ever sling hash or wait tables?" she asked.

"Well, not exactly." Deirdre explained about her mother's death and the fact that she had run the details of her father's social life, including banquets and cocktail parties for years. "It wasn't exactly 'hash-slinging,' " she said. "But I do have some passing understanding of what it takes to feed people."

"How 'bout working for me noons and evenings. That's when it gets kinda crowded and too busy for me and Julie to handle things by ourselves. Really could use the help."

Deirdre pondered the offer for about a second, then she stuck her hand out toward Sally. "You have a new employee," she declared.

Sam shifted uneasily in his chair. He and Andy had finished picking up all of the papers and had helped the Game and Fish boys load the stupefied moose into the back of their truck. It was long past time for him to go home, since it was Andy's shift officially. But Sam didn't usually do things officially.

He stared at the empty desk chair. He had been right in firing her, he told himself for the thousandth time. She was a green city lady who had no business in a town like Lodge Pole and certainly no business involved in dangerous police matters. If only she had shown more sense and less grit and had cowered behind Andy . . .

. She had saved the situation, he had to admit that. Sam pounded his fist on the desk. If she hadn't let out that war whoop—he smiled slightly at the memory—the moose could easily have chosen to attack the crowd instead. But, damn it all, if the tranquilizer hadn't worked, how could she have run in those damn high-heeled shoes? He was prepared to hightail it if necessary, but what would he have done with her? Slung her over his shoulder?

As he pondered it, it didn't seem like such a bad idea. At least under other circumstances. Carrying Deirdre Wilcox would be a pleasure . . .

But he'd never have a chance. Her show of icy temper when she had reentered the office to collect her things had dashed any hope that he might get to be friends with her, much less know her well enough to . . .

Sam brushed a hand over his eyes, trying to dismiss the image of her shapely form and large blue eyes. And that hair! Long and unbound as it had been this afternoon, it made him want to reach out and . . .

Damn! He strode over to the dispatch machine and called Andy. "I'm taking off," he told his officer. "Think I'll catch a bite at Sally's and then head home. You need me, call." Andy responded in the affirmative, saying that he was almost finished with Agatha Jaspers's fence and would be right in.

With one last glance around the empty, relatively tidy office, Sam took his coat and stepped out into the evening, reminding himself to get a new hat in the morning. The air was cold, but the wind had died down, and it felt refreshing on his face. He looked up and down the peaceful street, relishing the view. If he were in downtown Los Angeles right now, he reflected, the picture would certainly be different.

He strolled over to Sally's and entered, sniffing the aroma of fresh apple pie. His mouth began to water, and he admonished himself to eat lightly, leaving room for dessert.

He greeted everyone and took his usual place at the counter. Julie was rushing around, delivering orders, Sally was at her post at the fry stove and he could see another female form in the back part of the kitchen. "Hired some help?" he asked Sally, when she turned to smile at him.

"Sure did." There was an impish spark in her eyes. "Best darned little worker I ever had." She leaned over the stove and called through the opening into the back kitchen. "Dee, I got another customer. You want to come out and take his order, please."

Sam felt his jaw drop open when Sally's new "little worker" appeared with an order form in her slim hand. Deirdre smiled pleasantly at him and asked with professional politeness what he would like to order.

Sam couldn't speak. She had bound her long hair back in a ponytail, and a golden hairnet captured the tresses. She wore tailored slacks that showed off her figure even better than the skirt had, and the short-sleeved blouse she wore had ruffles down the front, accentuating her breasts.

"Chief . . ." she repeated. "What'll be your pleasure?"

He finally found his voice and automatically ordered the stew and a salad. He wasn't certain, but he thought he could detect a touch of innuendo in her choice of words. His pleasure, he decided, would be to reach across the counter and grab her perky ponytail, then . . .

"And to drink?" She scribbled his order quickly. Sally had forewarned her that he might be making an appearance this evening, since with all the excitement, he wouldn't be likely to cook for himself. She had planned to use the moment for revenge, but he was looking so confused and forlorn that she couldn't bring herself to gloat at him and to throw her new job in his face. Just be pleasant, she told herself. The man's had enough problems for one day.

"Milk," he said. "Make it a big one, please." She turned to go, but he reached out and touched her arm gently. "Deirdre, how in . . . ? I mean, what are you doing working *here*?"

"Sally asked me." The touch of his work-roughened fingers sent goosebumps up her arm and gave her a tingly feeling in the pit of her stomach. And she thought she saw a strange look in his eyes.

"You don't waste any time, do you."

She thought she detected a hint of admiration in his voice but dismissed it as due to her imagination. Or wishful thinking. For some reason, she wanted Sam Cassidy's admiration, although for the life of her, she couldn't understand why. Except for a brief interlude here and there, all the big man had done all day was cause her grief. Something she did not need.

"I'll place your order," she said in a brisk tone

designed to cut off further conversation. It worked. Sam's scarred hand fell from her arm and rested on the countertop, fingers tapping as if the man was nervous. Silly idea, she told herself. It would take an atomic bomb to shatter Sam Cassidy's reserve. She hurried into the back to fill his order.

Of course, she thought as she worked, he had seemed a bit on the flustered side this afternoon. His reaction to her action had been highly illogical. What if . . .?

Julie rushed into the kitchen. "They're backing up out there," the teenager said. "Please come help me after you get the chief's order filled." Deirdre replied that she would.

For the next hour, she found herself rushing busily from table to table. Clearly, Sally's café was popular, she decided, and a quick bite of the savory stew had shown her why. The prices were reasonable, and she imagined many working people preferred to come here rather than go home to fix dinner after a hard day. She herself was feeling more energized than ever, although she knew she should be dead tired. Maybe it was because Sam Cassidy hadn't left yet, she thought. He had eaten his meal, added apple pie and coffee to his order and then had sauntered over to a booth to visit with three other men. From the snatches of conversation she heard as she moved past them or refilled coffee cups, she learned that the main topic of the laconic discussion was the event with the moose. But whenever she was near, she noticed, Sam was silent.

Gradually, around eight, the café cleared out. People would be in bed early here, she deduced. Not much night life in a rural community that served mainly as a stopping point for tourists on their way to Jackson. Back in Washington, she thought, she might just be getting ready to go out. Quite a contrast.

Sally came into the back kitchen as Deirdre was cleaning up, her arms up to the elbows in hot, soapy water. "There's a customer wanting more coffee," she said. "You go on out and serve him. I'll finish up around here." Deirdre protested, but Sally insisted, saying that she could do the job faster, being used to it. Shrugging, Deirdre took the coffeepot and went out to find the customer.

Only one remained in the room. Sam Cassidy watched her approach, his green eyes slitted. "Bring a cup for yourself," he said. "You look like you could use it."

"Thank you very much," she answered with cool politeness. "But I work here. I don't . . ."

"Bring a cup." He sat up and gave her a hard look. "I told Sal I wanted to talk to you privately."

Deirdre hesitated. "Why?"

Making an annoyed sound, Sam got up, walked behind the counter, and picked up a clean cup. He returned and set it down on the table. Then he looked at her challengingly.

"You really are used to getting your own way, aren't you?" she snapped, thinking of what his reaction would be if she poured the coffee on his boots.

"Not all of the time." He indicated the bench. "Please, Deirdre. I'd like to talk to you."

His manner changed her mind. If he was willing to be halfway decent, then she would be boorish to keep on being prickly. Pouring the cups full, she put the pot on the table and sat down.

Sam sat back down, opposite her.

"Well . . ." Deirdre took a sip of her coffee. "What's on your mind, Chief?" She regarded him carefully. Without the flattening effect from his cowboy hat, his dark hair looked fuller. It shone in the bright light of the café, and she could see silver sprinkles at his temples and along his sideburns. He was, she decided, in his own unique way, very handsome.

Sam fiddled with his cup. Before she had sat down—when they were still at a Mexican stand-off—he had been certain that he only wanted to upbraid her again for her actions this afternoon and for working so hard this evening. If her father had sent her here to rest, the man had made a big mistake. And in a very strong way, he felt responsible for her, although he wasn't exactly certain why. She had removed the hairnet, and the ponytail hung freely down her back, a lock draping alluringly over her shoulder. His fingers itched to touch its silkiness.

"I . . ." he began, looking down at the table and wondering at his tonguetiedness. He'd never had trouble coming to the point with anyone before, much less a pretty woman. What was it about her that made him so . . . foolish?

"Sam . . ." She touched his hand, and he felt warmth from her fingers run all the way up his arm. "About this afternoon. I was wrong. I should have let you handle it. After all, you are the professional." A gleam lit her eyes. "Lodge Pole's very own Guardian Angel."

Deirdre tried not to grin when she saw his tanned cheeks bronze with a blush. Was he embarrassed, she wondered. Or just proud.

"Where'd you hear that one?" he mumbled, answering her question by the way he wouldn't meet her eyes.

"Tommy Edwards."

"Kid's got a big mouth." Sam looked up, and the electricity in his gaze caught her by surprise. She felt herself reddening at his frank scrutiny. "Am I wrong," he said, "or did I just hear a very plain and honest apology."

She nodded. "I acted on impulse today. It's something I rarely do, Sam. I was trained almost from birth to consider carefully every word and action."

"Politics?"

"I never wanted to embarrass my father. I always patterned my behavior to reflect well on him."

"You love him very much." Sam relaxed. The tension that had flared between them when he had ordered her to join him was gone. Maybe if he'd done a little less ordering and some more asking, things wouldn't be so . . . wrong.

"He's my daddy," she answered, smiling at him for the first time since their luncheon together. "Don't you feel that way about yours?"

"Both my parents are dead."

"I'm sorry, Sam." She put her hand on his. Impulse again, he wondered. She didn't strike him as the type of woman who went around touching men she didn't find appealing.

And he was finding her more appealing by the minute. When she had said the words about her father, her southern accent had been strong, and it charmed him down to his boot tips. What would she sound like if she were making love? he wondered, a tingle of desire touching him at the thought.

"It's okay," he replied, noting that she made no move to take her hand from his. "Dad died out in the orchard, working. It was the way he would have wanted to go. My mom . . ." He hesitated. No one else in Lodge Pole knew as much about his personal past as this woman sitting across from him had learned in a few brief moments. "My mom didn't go as easily," he said, looking down at her slim hand. She had repaired the broken and snagged nails and had removed all the polish. Tiny lines of dryness crisscrossed the pale skin, making the hand look more womanly, less painted doll.

Deirdre sensed that he didn't want to talk about his mother's death, so she changed the subject. "What kind of orchard did your father have?" she asked.

"Oranges." He smiled, and the skin beside his eyes crinkled. "It was hard work, but, oh, the smell of those trees in the spring when the blossoms were out . . ."

"I'm closing up, Sam, Dee." Sally's voice interrupted them, and Deirdre jerked her hand back. "When you leave, just make sure the door's tight."

Sam assured her he would. Then he turned back to Deirdre. "I told you I wanted to talk," he said, gazing directly into her eyes. "But suddenly I find that I want to be impulsive for a change."

"Impulsive?" She gave him a questioning look.

"After all we've been through today, I have no

right to ask this, Deirdre. But since I know you're free Saturday night, I wonder if you'd do me the honor of letting me take you out. We could drive over the pass into Jackson, have a good meal, maybe dance some, catch a movie." He smiled. "I could even show you a real cowboy bar that the tourists don't know about. It would be fun for you. What do you say?"

Amazed at his offer, Deirdre heard herself stammer a yes.

SIX

Deirdre lay sleepless in her bed. Four nights after Sam Cassidy had asked her for a date, she still had difficulty believing that the laconic, self-contained policeman had actually revealed a bit of his background and had shown that he was human enough to want her company. But then, she reflected, she had been wrong about many things in Lodge Pole.

Tommy Edwards was one. Since she only worked for Sally a few hours a day, she had taken the opportunity to seek the teenager out and offer to give him free diction lessons. To her amazement, Tommy had grinned shyly and refused politely, using perfect grammar.

"I'm able to talk perfectly well, Miss Wilcox," he had said. "We have a good school system and excellent teachers. But we also have our own dialect. You do, too." Deirdre asked him to explain, feeling foolish for making the offer. She had only wanted to help a likable young person. "You get this kind of softness when you aren't paying attention to what you're saying." He chuckled. "Kinda sound like your mouth's got some honey in it." Then he blushed.

Deirdre had apologized for assuming that he had a speech problem, confessing that when she had first arrived, she had a bad attitude toward being exiled to the small town. But, she said, she was beginning to relax and enjoy the slower pace.

"Does kinda grown on you," Tommy had replied.

Like Sam Cassidy, Deirdre thought, returning her mind to the present and thumping her pillow. The big policeman had been in to eat lunch and dinner every day since he had asked for the date, but he had left immediately after dining, making no effort to communicate with her in any special way—except by the gleam in his green eyes when she caught him staring at her unexpectedly. What, she wondered, would Saturday night bring? And was she ready to handle it?

Her social life back home had been easy enough to deal with. The boys and then men she had dated had smooth lines, but her wit had kept her clear of serious entanglements with the exception of the one she had told Sam about. Her one mistake in judging human character. But Sam was still a cipher, a mystery to her. How would he behave on a social occasion?

She forced her thoughts away from him and mused on the phone call she had received from her father earlier that evening. He had asked how her new job was working out, and without actually lying, she had convinced him that she was happy and was learning to take life a little easier. They had chatted for some time, and he filled her in on all the Capitol gossip, causing her to realize that there were fewer differences between Lodge Pole and Washington than she had thought at first. Her hours at Sally's had acquainted her with most of the townspeople, and she had decided that as a whole they were as fine, if not as polished, a group of human beings as she had ever met. Plain, honest, and cheerful. Even Sam seemed transformed when he walked in the door, kidding with friends and nodding a welcome to strangers. She was the only person who never ended up at the wrong end of one of his jokes. To her, Sam Cassidy was scrupulously polite. *Painfully* polite.

An odd sound brought her out of her reverie. She sat up and turned on the bedside light. The noise was vaguely familiar, sort of like air coming from a deflating balloon, but she knew it wasn't that. Curious, she padded barefoot in her nightgown through the house to the front door. Opening it, she stepped onto the wooden porch.

Moonlight lit the scene in front of the house, but she could see nothing but the tall pine trees that had given the town its name. "Is somebody there?" she called, realizing that she was experiencing none of the alarm she would have felt under similar conditions in the city. A huge, dark shape moved out of the shelter of the trees, and it took her only a fraction of a second to recognize that it was a man on horseback. It took even less time for her to realize that the man was Sam

"Evening . . ." he drawled, touching the brim of

his new hat. "Figured you might be asleep by now. Sorry if I woke you."

"It's okay." She lifted the long skirt of her gown and came down the steps. "I wasn't asleep. I heard your horse and was curious. It sounded like a dragon sneezing."

He chuckled, and his horse ducked its big dark head, making a chomping noise on the metal in its mouth. "A dragon, eh?" Sam said, patting the neck of the big animal. "You've just been upped a few notches in the animal kingdom, Licorice. What do you think about that, girl?"

"She's a *mare*?" Deirdre stepped onto the pine-needle-strewn yard and reached up to pat the horse's forehead. "Somehow, Sam, I see you as more the stallion type," she added teasingly. The mare's dark hair was coarse and warm to the touch.

"Stallion's too unreliable." His voice sounded as velvety as the animal's nose that Deirdre now stroked. "When I went looking for a horse," he continued, "I wanted one I could count on entirely. Licorice has proved out numerous times."

"I think she's beautiful." Deirdre scratched the mare's ears, and was rewarded with a nudge from the velvet nose. Sam laughed.

"She's asking you not to stop," he said. Then he held a hand out to her. "Want to take a short ride before you go to sleep?"

"Like this?" She pointed to her cotton nightgown and bare feet.

"No one's going to see you but me and Licorice, and Lic isn't much for gossiping."

Laughing at the sense of excitement and adventure

that rose in her, making her feel like a little girl again, Deirdre took his hand and let him pull her up to sit across his muscular thighs. Only then did she realize that she was no child and that the man who held her was probably the strongest she had ever met. And, in spite of his seemingly nonchalant attitude, he had expressed interest in her by asking her out for Saturday night. Where, she wondered as she put her arms around his neck for support, would the ride lead to?

He clicked to the mare, and Deirdre felt his thigh move slightly. The horse turned obediently and headed into the woods. Deirdre moved closer to Sam as they entered the pines.

"I've done some riding before," she said conversationally, trying not to notice how warm he felt through the thin nightgown. He smelled of leather and spice and horse, and the wool sweater he wore felt soft over the hardness of his muscles. "Your horse does seem very well trained."

"She is." In the moonlight she saw the flash of a grin. "Unlike some females I know."

"Sam . . ." she said in a warning tone.

"Just kidding." He held the reins in one hand and reached up to push her head gently down on his shoulder. "Relax now. This'll make you sleep like a baby." His arm encircled her waist, securing her to him.

They rode in peaceful silence for a while, and she found that the gentle rhythm of the mare's gait did have a relaxing effect. She settled even more closely to Sam.

Sam noted the movement as he had noted everything else about her since she had come out onto the porch. The long cotton gown was hardly sexy, but it gave her an appealing enticingness that no lacy negligee could have. Her long hair hung like a silky cloud around her shoulders, and a stray strand or two was teasing his neck. She fit against him as if she had always been supposed to be there, and the sensation made him struggle for self-control.

He hadn't meant to waken her. It was his habit at night to give the town one last patrol on horseback. Give him a chance to exercise Licorice and to sort out his thoughts. And his thoughts had been troublesome lately. Since he had asked the lady in his arms out for Saturday night.

Still two nights away, he found that he had very mixed emotions about the event. She was used to sophisticated entertainment from men who moved in her world of politics and culture. Sam had no illusions about himself. He knew ladies liked him, but beyond the obvious, did he have anything to offer Deirdre? And why should it matter to him? She was here for the summer only. He smiled grimly to himself. So she was safe to date, since she posed no permanent temptation. That was the last thing he wanted. Solitude suited him.

But he knew he was looking forward with unusual eagerness to their date. A simmering feeling of excitement that hadn't bothered him in years. Deirdre sighed, and a wash of emotion ran through him. She was so soft. Light in his arms and against his body like a dream. But the warmth that radiated from her was real. As real as the tantalizing teasing of her hair on his neck.

"Getting sleepy?" he asked, hearing his own voice sound unusually gentle. She shifted, and smiled up at him.

"I'm relaxed," she whispered. "But I'm not very sleepy."

That did it! Sam gave Licorice the signal to stop. Deirdre continued to look up at him, the moonlight making her eyes jewels in her pale, delicate face. Slowly, he lowered his head until his lips covered hers.

Deirdre knew the kiss was coming the moment she looked at him. In spite of the peacefulness of their ride, there had also been a tension in him that she could feel, and when she saw the light of desire in his eyes, she suddenly knew what that tension had been about.

His kiss was gentle, tender, and unintrusive, but it left her tingling and wanting more. Sam, however, pulled away.

"Sorry," he muttered. "I didn't ask you out here for a come-on. Don't know what got into me." He tugged the reins, and Licorice turned obediently back in the direction of her house.

For a moment, she wasn't sure how to react. Sam Cassidy had certainly wanted to do more than kiss her so lightly, Deirdre was sure of that. So then why . . . ?

He was making his mare go at a fast walk, unlike the slow ambling that had preceded the kiss. Almost, she decided, as if he couldn't get back to dump her quickly enough. Pride warred with logic. She knew enough about men to be positive that Sam found her desirable, but she had been through enough with him already to feel too stubborn to help him out, to encourage him. When they reached her place, she slid from his lap without his assistance and marched up the wooden steps before turning around and thanking him.

"I enjoyed the ride," she said in a brisk tone. "The kiss wasn't bad, either. But I won't accept your silly apology, since I wanted to kiss you, too. Goodnight, Sam."

Sam watched as she turned her back, squared her shoulders, and entered her doorway with all of the unruffled dignity of a queen. Every cell in his body ached to dismount, charge up the stairs, and bust through the closed door. Then . . .

Then give her the kiss she deserved—deserved because of her womanly beauty, her strong spirit, her ability to take an awkward situation and put it to her own advantage. Hell, he wanted to kiss her because he *wanted* to.

Licorice began to sidestep, and he knew she was feeling his pent-up tension. But he watched until all the lights went out in Deirdre's house before turning his mare in the direction of an open meadow where they were both able to let off steam with a long gallop.

The next morning, Deirdre reviewed events in her mind as she dressed. Sam didn't have any reason to like her other than the fact that she wasn't ugly. She had been forced on him by political higher-ups. She had interfered with the moose situation. She had proved she didn't need him by immediately getting another job after he had fired . . . No, after she had quit. So why the moments when she sensed he wanted to draw close to her, emotionally as well as physically? The lunch they had shared the first day. The way he had opened up about his childhood that night at Sally's café. His asking her out for a date, for goodness' sake! Then last night, after several days of practically ignoring her . . . She pressed her palms to her head. Sam Cassidy was one strange man.

But, she had to admit, she liked him in spite of his quirks. He clearly had the open admiration of the community of Lodge Pole, and that spoke volumes to her of his professional ability. She could appreciate the kind of wisdom it must take for a policeman to command that sort of positive respect anywhere, especially in a small community where secrets were probably almost as nonexistent as they were in the political community back in Washington.

Next time, she promised herself, Sam Cassidy tried to avoid talking about the reasons he had stuck himself up here in the middle of nowhere, he was going to find himself at the rapier end of her inquisitive tongue. And next time he kissed her. . . !

Sam slammed the phone receiver down so hard that the ancient instrument almost shattered. *Damn* the woman anyhow, he thought. Her mere presence in Lodge Pole had already caused him almost as much trouble as his own foolhardy behavior that had led him to leave Los Angeles. He slammed his fist down on the table, causing a pile of papers to tumble to the floor.

No, he thought as he regarded the mess with distaste, that wasn't really true. He was blowing the situation way out of perspective, just as the public, press, and finally the Department had with his stupid heroics. It was emotional, not logical. He was allowing this thing with Deirdre to get to him because from the first moment she had walked through his office door he had sensed the specialness, the uniqueness of her. He smiled, remembering the softness of her lips against his, the sweet scent of her body and hair mingling with the pine-tinged night air.

It wasn't Deirdre's fault that too many people cared about her. Including himself, he had to admit. The only thing he didn't like about having to ask her to come back to work for him was the fact that he'd been *ordered* to do it. The earlier call that morning from Senator Wilcox had forced him to admit that Deirdre had lasted for less than one day in his employ. The second one from the governor had politely suggested that the young lady be given another chance. That her abilities would be better utilized in his office instead of being wasted in a café. Sam groaned and put his face in his hands.

He had, he decided, only a limited capacity to obey superiors, and it must have all been used up during his time in the service and with the L.A.P.D. He remembered the sense of satisfaction he'd felt when he had told his captain that he was resigning and taking the job here in Lodge Pole. He had disobeyed direct orders from the man, and his actions had saved lives. Had injured no one but himself. He had been *right,* but the captain would have died rather than admit it. Resigning had contained a shade of revenge for the disciplinary action taken against him, and he had learned from the few friends he'd kept in contact with that the press had vilified the captain and the entire Department for letting him go after . . .

Enough reminiscing, he scolded himself. Now his job was to work up enough guts to take himself down to Sally's and ask . . . plead with Deirdre to come back. The idea almost made him feel like running away, but he had sworn to himself that when he had come to Lodge Pole, he had reached home ground No running from here. Even if it meant a small sacrifice of pride to please a politico.

Sam stood and picked up the dropped papers. Then he took his hat from the rack, leaving the windbreaker he'd worn to work. Now that June was almost here, the days were warm at noon. He buckled on his gun, grinning at the thought that he might have to arrest her to force her back to the station. *That* would give the townsfolk something to talk about.

Deirdre rubbed her forearm across her perspiring forehead. At noon, back in the rear kitchen, Sally's place was a steam bath, but she insisted on taking her turn. Sally and Julie were working just as hard up front, and Deirdre was determined not to shirk. She lifted the lid of a huge pot of chili and stirred the steamy, aromatic mixture, making certain that she cleared the bottom of the pot so that none burned.

Her days and evenings at Sally's, she reflected, had taught her a great deal. All her labors in the past had been mostly cerebral, but here it was definitely physical. Oh, she had to keep track of orders and remember tasks like she was performing now, but it mainly involved her hands and body. Good for a change, and it made her appreciate people like Sally who did it all of their lives.

But she had to admit that the drudgery was beginning to pall. She had bitten her tongue to keep from reorganizing Sally's system of cooking, knowing that while she could streamline things, this was Sally's life, and her interference, however well meant, would not be appreciated. A twinge of longing for another crack at Sam's station hit her.

Oh, no, she thought. She'd managed to keep her change of jobs secret from her father, and she had no intention of getting Sam in trouble. Her relationship with the big policeman was weird enough without outside intervention.

Weird. That was a strange way to describe it, she mused. But it fit. She set the lid down firmly and turned, chili-dripping stirring spoon still in her hand.

"Whoa!" Sam's big body blocked her way. Apparently he had been standing close behind her while she was ministering to the chili. Why? she wondered. And for how long?

"I didn't know you were there," she said, keeping her tone cool but friendly. "Sorry I almost bumped into you."

"My own fault." He held up his hands in mock surrender. "The chili smelled so good, I just couldn't resist getting close."

He was smiling, but something about his expression made her suspicious. If he wanted to smell chili, why hadn't he taken his usual place at the counter and ordered some. And there was a look in his eyes that reminded her suddenly of a desperate lobbiest trying to get an appointment with her father. Sam Cassidy was up to something, she decided.

"If you want a bowl," she said, moving past him to check the big coffee urn, "just tell me, and I'll bring you a bowl. But scoot out of here, please. It's hard enough to keep on top of things without having to trip over Angels."

Sam winced inside at what was clearly a deliberate jibe. "I'm no angel, Deirdre," he said, following her as she moved around the hot room. "I thought I proved that last night."

"Ha!" She jabbed a fork at a slab of ham and started sawing slices off the meat. "I've had better kisses from my cousins."

Sam narrowed his eyes. She wasn't looking at him—all of her attention was on the ham. Today her hair was braided, and encircled her head like a golden crown. But she wore no makeup, and with the sweat gleaming on her skin and staining the simple blouse she wore with her jeans, she looked like a blend of both aspects of Cinderella: the drudge and the princess. In short, she looked delicious.

"That sounds suspiciously like a challenge," he said. Before he had come into the back kitchen, he had told Sally that he wanted to speak to Deirdre in private, so he knew that they would be uninterrupted for at least a few minutes. Maybe he had been too much of a gentleman for the lady.

Deirdre set down the fork and carving knife. The room was sultry enough without his suggestive comment, and she started to turn and give him a verbal lashing.

But Sam's hands caught her shoulders. His mouth covered hers, and she was slowly pulled into a state of physical pleasure that melted into rapture. The kiss last night had given her no indication that Sam Cassidy could work such wonders with his lips and tongue.

He kept her away from his body, but he teased and tantalized her until she felt all sense of the hot, steamy kitchen disappear, and there was only her and Sam. Hungrily, she began to respond, tasting the specialness of him with her own tongue.

It was magic. As if they had been lovers for years, she thought muzzily. He knew all the right places to touch, and she could tell from the increased rate of his breathing that she was doing well for him, too. *What is going on?* she wondered.

After a time, Sam broke the kiss. Deirdre gazed up at him, ready for more, but then she saw the expression on his face shift from one of desire to confusion and then harden to its usual stoical stoniness. ,

''Actually, Deirdre . . .'' he said, his voice indicating no passion at all. ''What I really came here for was to ask you to come back and work for me again.''

SEVEN

Deirdre stared, trying to read truth somewhere in his green eyes, but all she saw was evasiveness. Was it the kiss? Or the unbelievable offer of anther chance at his office? What was Sam covering up? Feelings? Or something less pleasant?

"Why?" She threw the word at him, and she wasn't surprised when he released her shoulders and turned, running his hand through his hair. Body language, she thought. Sam Cassidy had a problem.

"Because I do need you to get the place in shape," he said, still not looking at her. "I acted impulsively when I fired you, and I think you should have another chance to—"

Deirdre swore. She rarely lost her temper, but this big liar was making her do it. "I quit, remember," she shouted. "And you don't want anyone to do *anything* with your precious office. You just want to be in charge. The big cheese. The Chief! The Guardian Angel! Besides," she added, "I already have a job, thank you very much."

Sam turned and glared at her, his eyes emerald fire. "A job that can be filled by any number of people in this town. But I need someone used to administration. To taking on responsibility."

"Oh?" She folded her arms across her chest. "As I recall, when I did that, I got canned."

"Damn it, Deirdre!" Sam started to wind up for further argument but was interrupted by the bustling entrance of Sally.

"Time's up, Sam," she said, grinning. "I need Dee for at least the rest of the lunch hour. You two can carry on your lover's quarrel later. It was interesting to listen to, but I think some of the customers are getting indigestion."

"We aren't lovers," Deirdre snapped. She picked up the knife and sliced viciously at the ham.

Sam started to reply, but Sally caught his eye. Her expression was one of sympathy, but she gestured with her head that he'd best leave. Muttering under his breath, he did just that, taking the back way out so that he wouldn't have to face the audience in the café.

Deirdre, however, was not so fortunate. Sally insisted that she had been stuck in the kitchen for more than her allotted time and shooed her out to take orders for a while. When she entered the dining area, many of the locals broke into applause. Covering her extreme embarrassment, she grinned and gave them a little bow.

"Way to go, Miss Deirdre," the thin man she recognized as Tommy Edwards's father, John, said.

"Didn't think there was a soul in this town could dress down Sam Cassidy like you just done. You fried him so hot, I bet his skin's red."

Deirdre smiled and lifted her chin. "I did my best, Mr. Edwards. And I apologize if I offended anyone." A chorus of negatives reassured her that, in fact, her recitation had entertained everyone. Relieved, she picked up the order blanks and started to work.

As the rest of the noon hour passed, she began to muse on the events. Sam's kiss. His offer. The warm feeling she had gotten when the locals had been so tickled at her treatment of him. The feeling . . . the feeling that she was suddenly one of them. No longer an outsider from the East. Even John's slaughtering of the English language hadn't grated on her as it had done in the past.

When the café cleared out a little past one, Sally signaled her to join her in one of the booths. Puzzled, Deirdre obeyed, although she felt reluctant to leave the cleaning up and preparation for dinner to Julie alone.

"He wants you back, don't he," Sally stated, looking directly at Deirdre. "That's what he came to ask you."

"I don't intend to go." Deirdre folded her arms across her chest. "You need me here."

"Look, Dee . . ." Sally gestured with her large, reddened hands. "I think you and me, we're friends. Right?"

"Of course." Deirdre unfolded her arms. "That's why . . ."

"That's why you're going back to Sam, honey."

The old woman's eyes glowed. "Maybe I shouldn'ta said that about you two having a lover's quarrel, but I got to confess that I poked my head in earlier when you two was kissing. Left right away, but I know a kiss that means something when I see one."

Deirdre felt herself blushing. "Sally, I—"

"Just go talk to him. Sam's a dark man, and he don't let folks see too far inside. But for the instant I saw him when he was holding you, Dee, I saw such tenderness, such . . . Oh, I don't know, honey. I sure ain't one to be giving out advice about romance, but I think you ought to go to him. Like I heard him say, I *can* get another helper. Unless you just plain hate his guts, which I don't think's possible, you get yourself down the street to the station. Sam Cassidy *needs* you."

Sam started in surprise when the call signal went off on his walkie-talkie. After his encounter with Deirdre, he had glumly patroled the streets on foot, hoping that his emotions would sort themselves out while he walked. All that had happened so far was that he could feel his insides tangle into tighter knots. Why had he made such a damn fool of himself? Kissing her, then getting into an argument like that where half the town could hear them? *Sam*, he told himself, *you'd better watch it. This entire situation could get seriously out of control.* But as he flicked the switch on his receiver, he remembered how sweet she had tasted and how after only a moment's hesitation she had returned his kiss so deliciously.

"Cassidy here," he said into the machine. "What do you need, Andy?"

"You got company, Chief," Andy's voice replied, sounding tinny and thin over the airwaves. Sam thought he caught a touch of something else in his officer's tone.

"Company?" he asked. "What kind?"

This time, Andy gave an unprofessional sigh. "The kind of company I'd curl up and die for, Chief. She's . . ." His voice was cut off, and Sam thought he heard a few words from a familiar female whipping out at his officer. Then:

"Cassidy, this is Deirdre. If it's not too much trouble, I'd appreciate it if you'd come back here and let Andy finish patrol. We have some business to discuss."

"You're going to . . . ?"

"Just get back here!" The radio contact went dead.

Sam stood for a moment, staring at his receiver. Then he quickly hooked it back on his belt and headed at a fast walk back to the station.

She was waiting for him, and the moment he entered the station and saw her, Sam knew he was in for it. She had come fully armed. Andy leaned against the wall, a stupid grin on his face. Sam scowled and signaled him to leave. It was liable to get messy, and he wanted no witnesses. Still grinning, Andy obeyed.

Deirdre sat in the station's seat of power—his own—forcing him to make the choice between rudely asking her to get up or standing as if he were a prisoner and she the interrogator. He vacillated between anger and admiration. She knew the rules of the power game all right.

She also knew some other rules and had clearly put them to good use. Her hair was down, kinky-curly from having been up in braids, but she had somehow managed to look both incredibly sexy and at the same time ladylike. He could tell that she had bathed. The station office was fragrant with a delicate floral scent, and her face was made up with a sophistication he hadn't seen before. She looked like a movie-screen goddess. She wore a beige business suit, but the pale rose blouse under the tailored jacket looked like lingerie. Sam felt his palms start to sweat.

Deirdre studied him. He was the most difficult man to read she had ever met. She knew that her "special effects" had to be working on him. But all she could see in those glacier-green eyes was impatience. And perhaps a touch of anger that she had chosen to sit in the "cat-bird"'s seat, putting him at a physical disadvantage.

However, she had to grudgingly grant him a point when he crossed the room, took the chair from the other desk, and planted it right next to her. He straddled it, resting his arms on the back, and gave her a thin smile.

"You're coming back," he said in a tone that indicated no doubts.

"I'm here to negotiate," she countered, looking at him levelly.

A puzzled frown crossed his face. "What's to negotiate? I filled you in on Monday. This is Friday, and nothing's changed."

"Oh, really?" She arched an eyebrow. "Chief

Cassidy, I would have thought your vision was a bit less limited."

Sam felt a twist of annoyance in his midsection. She was playing him like a hooked trout, and he didn't like the feeling one bit. "What do you mean?" he snapped.

She clasped her hands together and placed them on the desk. She looked, he decided, every inch a woman of quality—breeding, brains, and beauty. The sweaty, chili-stirring drudge who had taunted him into kissing her must still lurk somewhere under the highly polished surface, but for the life of him, Sam couldn't see her. He wondered if he'd ever have the nerve to kiss *this* version of Deirdre Wilcox. Another challenge, he thought. But this time it wasn't vocalized. Just packaged in a sophisticated shell.

"What I mean, Sam, . . ." she was saying, "is that you and I have got to be perfectly honest with one another."

"Fine with me." What was she leading up to?

"You don't really want me back, do you."

The bluntness of her statement caught him off guard, and he knew that his carefully cultivated neutral expression slipped. He took a deep breath and plunged. "I want you back, Deirdre. But you've got to know that I wouldn't have asked you on my own."

Deirdre barely suppressed a gasp of astonishment. Not only had the stony expression been replaced by one of vulnerable confusion, but she never expected him to admit the truth so quickly. She had come prepared to fight for every detail.

"My father called?" she asked. Sam nodded. "And the—"

"Governor," he concluded for her. He stood and started to pace the room. "I should have told you earlier, but I just guess I wanted you to think that I'd come to my senses without having to get kicked in the behind." He turned and looked at her. "Anyway, didn't that kiss in the kitchen give you some idea that I'd prefer having you nearer than halfway across town?"

Deirdre smiled. "Town's not very big, Sam."

Taking a change, he held out his hand to her. "Sometimes, between some people, even the distance of a few inches is too far."

Instinctively, Deirdre started to take his hand, but pulled back before they made contact. "Sam . . ." she said softly. "You know this is only temporary. That I'll be leaving in the fall."

"I know." He still held out his hand. "But I thought you wanted honesty. If I try to pretend you don't move me as a man, I wouldn't be truthful."

She looked at him, seeing the warmth in his eyes, and believed him. "Let me blot my lipstick," she said, suddenly feeling shy. "I'd hate to ruin your reputation by getting makeup on your uniform." She fumbled in her purse for a tissue.

"Who gives a hang for my reputation!" He reached down and drew her into his arms. For a moment, Deirdre gazed up into his face. Then slowly, tenderly, Sam Cassidy started to kiss her.

Deirdre wound her arms around his neck, feeling the sweet rush of desire fill her. For a man so big and strong, he held and caressed her gently, almost as if he feared she would break. For now, she thought dreamily, she'd let him have his way. But if he kept on like this much longer, Sam Cassidy was going to discover that she was hardly made of delicate china. Melding her body to his, she lifted one hand to stroke the thick softness of his hair.

Sam felt lost in the wonderment of the feelings that welled up in him at her touch. They had agreed to be honest with each other, but he wasn't sure that he even knew himself what was happening to him. Deirdre Wilcox had many facets—he already knew that. What he wasn't prepared for was her sweet softness and the pleasure that her caress brought him. He felt desire, but not as he had in the past. This had something else in it. Something . . . elusive, but something that made him yearn to put a name to it.

Touching her carefully, ready to stop if she protested, he moved his hand from her waist, up her side, and cupped one silk-clad breast with his hand. She seemed to welcome the caress, because she pushed against his palm, inviting him. He felt both shaky inside and powerful as her flesh swelled in his hand.

Deirdre suppressed a gasp. Her body reacted to his more intimate touch like tinderwood to a flame. She was out of control, completely at the mercy of the strong man holding her and willing for him to do anything to her. Panic warred with desire as she struggled inwardly for the willpower she had always been able to use to keep men where *she* wanted them. Right now, she knew that Sam Cassidy was in charge. The Angel had slipped past her emotional defenses somehow, and she was literally putty in his hands, a condition she found frightening.

But before she could do anything to change the situation, Sam broke the embrace. She could tell from his rapid breathing and the ruddiness of his tanned cheeks that he had been moved as well. But there was a gleam of triumph behind the warmth in his eyes, and that made her mad.

"This really isn't a very good way to start a professional relationship," she said, pushing away from him.

"No, it's not." His expression was entirely serious, but she could see amusement in his eyes. "I apologize for behaving honestly."

"Very funny."

Sam shrugged. "Well, Miss Wilcox, that's what you said you wanted, wasn't it?"

Deirdre caught herself just before she began to sputter in frustrated rage. He had her nicely trapped by her own words. She would have to concede the point to him.

Sam wanted to say something to ease the tension grown between them—wanted to restore them to that moment when they had been so close, but he knew that she deserved to simmer in the juices of her own making. She had obviously dressed to seduce. That he had followed up on the invitation was her own fault. She had tried to dominate him, and he wasn't having that. Not in his own station.

Although her lips and body tingled pleasurably from his caresses, Deirdre forced herself to assume a cool, businesslike manner. "Let me clarify myself, please," she said, straightening her jacket and blouse.

"Our official relationship is that of employer and employee. That's the area I was referring to when I spoke of honesty. As for the other . . ."

He smiled, looking like he knew a special secret. "Why don't we just let nature take its course on that, Miss Wilcox."

She nodded abruptly. "Fine." Pushing back a sense of disappointment that he hadn't tried to kiss her again, she mentally berated herself for even *thinking* she wanted to go all jelly-fleshed in his arms again. She glanced down at her wristwatch. "I have a few hours left to start in. Is it all right with you, Chief?"

"Certainly." Again, the gleam in the eyes.

"Very well."

The next few hours were the hardest Deirdre could remember having lived through emotionally. Not that they were painful. But they *were* horribly embarrassing. She moved around the office, gathering papers and sorting them on her desk in a preliminary filing system, and Sam Cassidy sat at his desk. Watching her. He didn't even pretend to do any work, and she could actually *feel* his gaze follow her around the room. They exchanged a few sentences now and then when she needed to know the value or meaning of a particular item, but the tone of the conversation was just businesslike. The contrast between his quiet, neutral voice and the constant *watching* slowly drove her to the point where she felt she would burst with frustration.

Once the phone rang, jarring her frazzled nerves and almost causing her to scatter carefully organized papers all over the floor. Sam answered, and Deirdre watched him out of the corner of her eye as he listened to the speaker at the other end. He made sparse responses to what he was hearing, but she could tell that he didn't like the message. A frown appeared on his face, and his fingers started to tap the desktop. Finally, he muttered a thanks and hung up.

She itched to know what the call had been about but hesitated to ask, figuring that she'd get no satisfactory answer. At least it had the effect of distracting him from her momentarily. Now she watched him.

Sam stared off into space, the frown causing his full lips to turn downward and deepening the cleft in his chin. She saw him in profile and realized afresh how ruggedly handsome the man was. The dark hair, tanned skin, sculptured features. . . . Momentarily, weakness flooded her, and she wanted to go put her arms around him, thinking that perhaps her touch would ease whatever problem was on his mind.

But that, she told herself, was utter foolishness. She had declared the terms and she had to abide by them, no matter what her feelings were. Sam was the professional lawman, and she was a professional organizer. He had his job, and she had hers. Reluctantly, she returned to it.

"I'm going for a walk," he said suddenly. "I'd appreciate it if you'd stay here until I get back. Mind?"

"Of course not." She gave him a pleasant smile but was disappointed when he seemed not to notice. "I've enough here to keep me busy until Christmas."

A shadow of a smile did turn his lips then.

"That'd be nice, Deirdre. Too bad we can't arrange it."

Long after he had closed the door behind him, Deirdre stared at it. What had he meant by that last statement? Just a pleasantry? Of course, that's all it could have been. And yet . . .

For the first time, she thought about the possibility of staying in Lodge Pole longer than just for the summer. The sensation the idea brought to her was similar to sliding between winter-chilly sheets and then having them gradually warm up around her. She had many reasons to go back and few to stay. But the notion wouldn't leave her alone. It kept buzzing around in her head while she worked until she thought she would go crazy.

Furiously, she attacked the file cabinet, emptying the drawers and adding the papers to the stacks growing like stalagmites on her desk. The bottom drawer was stuck, and she had difficulty opening it but finally managed to jerk it free.

It was empty except for a large manilla envelope that was unlabeled. She took it out, making a mental note to ask Tommy Edwards to bring her some oil for the drawer sliders. Then she opened the envelope, planning on adding its contents to her collection.

But when she looked at the newspaper clippings inside, she knew that these belonged nowhere in her official files. Headlines screamed "Hero Cop"; "Officer Risks Life for Hostages"; "L.A.P.D. Unjustified in Treatment of Hero." A younger but more careworn Sam Cassidy looked at her from the newspages. Deirdre scanned one article, horrified at what she was reading. Sam had deliberately disobeyed a superior officer during a hostage situation. Had put aside his weapon and had walked toward the gunman, offering to exchange himself for the civilian victims. The report was confused after that detail, but the outcome of the situation was that Sam had sustained a gunshot wound but had captured the gunman. He had also been disciplined severely by the Department. Hastily, she stuffed the article back into the envelope and returned it to the lower drawer. Now she understood much more about Sam Cassidy, but she doubted he would appreciate knowing that she had found out the probable reason he had left the city for a place where he could make his own judgments and carry them out. She had just returned to the desk when the door opened and Sam and Andy walked in together.

EIGHT

"My God," Andy blurted. "You told me she was back in service, Chief, but you didn't tell me she was gonna do a year's work in one evening."

"Time to quit, Deirdre," Sam said to her, ignoring Andy's remark. "The kid here's in charge for the night. Let's go get some dinner."

"Oh, not at Sally's!" Deirdre laughed nervously. "I don't think I could face the people there after the scene we put on this noon."

"What scene?" Andy's expression showed intense curiosity.

"None of your business," Sam said in a good-natured tone. "You've got your orders now. Keep alert, and call me if you need anything."

Deirdre saw a look exchanged between the two men. Something was afoot, and she wondered what it was, but she was certain that any questions would get the same rebuke that Andy had received. Then Sam smiled at her.

"I wasn't thinking of taking you to Sally's," he said, handing her jacket to her. "She's a good cook, but I know of a better one, when he decides he's in the mood. Like rainbow trout?"

A little dazed by the entire day and what she had just discovered about his past, it took her a moment to realize that he was inviting her to his home for dinner. Finally, she stammered an affirmative and let Sam help her on with her jacket.

His home, located about a mile from town, was little more than a rustic cabin with a corral and stable in the back yard. But when Deirdre stepped inside, she saw that it was warm and cozy, decorated with a clearly masculine artistic style. The walls were paneled with wood and the floor was polished wood, bare except for strategically placed woven rugs. Fabric art as well as western-motif paintings hung on the walls, and she hurried over to study them, expressing her delight at the quality of his collection.

"Some of these are real showpieces," she declared. "Where on earth did you get them?"

"Roundabouts." Sam took her jacket. "During the summer, this whole area becomes a kind of artist colony. Especially over in Jackson. You can pick up some real bargains if you know what to look for."

"And apparently you do." Deirdre moved on to study another painting.

"I know what I like," he jibed, enjoying the sound of her laughter at his use of the old phrase.

The evening passed pleasantly. Deirdre was astonished at Sam's cooking skills, but reminded herself that a bachelor had two choices: eat out constantly or develop his own talents. Clearly, Sam had chosen the latter.

After dinner, they sat drinking coffee on the sofa in the main room. They talked, sharing bits and pieces of their pasts, but Deirdre noted that although he had removed his gunbelt, Sam had kept his uniform on, and there was an underlying current of edginess about him that she could tell had nothing to do with her presence. In fact, she suspected that he was calmed by her. Whenever she launched into another anecdote about life in politics, he looked more relaxed. He told her a few stories about his past career in L.A. but never touched on the event that she had inadvertently discovered documented in the envelope. Was he ashamed of it? she wondered. And if so, why keep the clippings? Eventually, she hoped, he would volunteer his side of the story, so she kept quiet about it. But about another matter, she felt free to question him.

"Since you've demonstrated your talents as a cook and I already know about your kissing ability, do you mind a personal question?" She leaned her head back on the sofa and looked at him.

Sam grinned. "Could it be why there's no Mrs. Cassidy?"

"My very words."

He regarded her. "Never met the right woman. In my profession, it isn't difficult to have enough girlfriends. Just the uniform draws them. But I'm afraid I'm a confirmed bachelor."

"Sam, don't tell me you've never been in love."

He shook his head. "I've been momentarily crazy about this one or that one but never met anyone I knew could be to me like my mom was to my father." He put his cup down on the coffee table. "He was life to her. When he died, I think that's when she began to go. It just took longer."

Impulsively, Deirdre put her hand on his shoulder. "Excuse me, Sam, but could it be that you just don't want to be that vulnerable? My father suffered after Mom died, but he went on with his life and is doing just fine."

"Amateur psychology?" He seemed amused.

"Unbreakable habit," she admitted. "I suppose it comes from learning how to size people up from watching my dad. I just can't resist trying to find out what makes a person tick."

He narrowed his eyes. "You could be dangerous to have around if a man had secrets to keep."

"Do you?" she challenged.

He took the cup from her hand and set it beside his on the table. "You want to know my deepest, darkest secret?" he asked. She nodded, feeling a glow start deep inside. This wasn't going to have anything to do with his past, but she eagerly awaited his words anyway.

"I find," he murmured, touching his lips to her cheek, "that I'm momentarily *insane* about a certain senator's daughter who's much too bright for her own good." His hand caressed her hair.

"Is insane better than crazy?" She put her arm around his neck. They were out of the office, a kind of friendship was being established, and, as Sam had said that afternoon, nature was taking its course. She felt no inner restraints.

"Much better," he whispered, brushing her lips

with his. "It's even better than demented, which is what I am for finding you so delicious."

"Now I'm an after-dinner candy?" She teased the soft hair at the back of his neck.

"Let's see." His lips closed over hers. Unresisting, Deirdre opened to him. No matter what went on between them otherwise, when they kissed, all that mattered was the magic. She ran her hand over his back, enjoying the feel of his muscles. His very size and strength had the effect of making her feel safe and secure, even though he was still a relative stranger to her and certainly had secrets he was unwilling to share. She reveled in his touch.

Sam held himself back with great difficulty. She was soft and yielding in his arms, but he had several reasons for limiting intimacy tonight, not the least of which was the potential trouble the phone call had warned him about. His other reasons . . . well, he decided to think about them later. For now, there was the sweetest woman in the world in his arms.

She moved, bringing them closer together, and Sam felt his desire for her rise with a suddenness that amazed him. The most intimate thing he had done with her so far was to lightly touch one breast that afternoon, but here he was, more inflamed with passion than he could ever remember.

"Deirdre . . ." he whispered, tasting the silky skin along the side of the throat. "The way you make me feel . . ."

"I know," she replied, her voice low and husky. "I feel it, too. Sam, where did this come from?"

He took her face in his hands and gazed into her eyes. "I don't know," he told her. Her skin was so soft against his rough palms. "We're about as different as two people could be, but there's *something* . . ."

"How are we different?" she asked, her eyes still warm but suddenly analytical. "Except for the obvious," she added, smiling and drawing one finger across his chest, raising goosebumps over his entire body.

"Well . . ." he began. "I live here, and you—"

"Live here, too." Deirdre watched his expression. The man was clearly suffering from some inner struggle. Could it be that his feelings for her were stronger than he cared for them to be? She wouldn't call what she felt for him love yet, but he certainly had aroused a deep affection in her heart or she wouldn't be sitting here alone with him. From what he had told her, he had kept his emotional distance from his lady friends. Was he having trouble doing that with her?

"You won't live here for long." He frowned and withdrew from the embrace. "Your life is in the kind of city I ran from."

"Ran? Or made an intelligent decision to leave for your own well-being?" She watched him closely.

Sam smiled wryly. "Damn, but I'd like to see you interrogate a suspect. You know just how to ask the question that might make the poor sap unload his story."

She took his hand. "Sam, kiss me again, and then tell me another reason why we're different. Because the first one won't wash. Remember that I came out here for *my* well-being, too."

He looked at her with suspicion smoking in his

eyes, and she worried that he would ask if she had snooped in his private file. But then the look faded, and he drew her in for a warm embrace. "I can't resist you, Deirdre. Even when I get the feeling I should trust you as far as I could throw Licorice."

She laughed and caressed his bicep. "That might be a fair distance. Poor horse." She teased her fingers up to his lips.

"Poor horse, my—" The ringing of the telephone interrupted him. Sam felt the pent-up passion fade as he reached for the receiver. He had hoped that Salters had been able to keep the lid on, but apparently the old man hadn't had the control of his Three Diamond boys that he used to. Andy's quickly spoken words confirmed his fears. He hung up and swung off the sofa.

"Gotta go," he said, reaching into his pocket and tossing her the keys to his car. "Some trouble downtown. Drive yourself home and stay there. I'll take Lic. She'll get me there as quickly as the Jeep would." He kissed her quickly and ran out the kitchen door.

Deirdre sat stunned for a moment. It was long enough for to hear hoofbeats disappearing into the night. He must not even have taken time to saddle the mare, she thought. Then another thought twisted her midsection.

She turned and saw his gunbelt hanging on the hall tree by the door. Sam was unarmed!

Quickly, she marshaled her thoughts. She dialed the station and got no answer, so Andy must be on his way to back Sam up. But if the trouble were

something beyond the skills of the younger officer
. . . She dialed another number.

"Hello, Sally. This is Deirdre. I have a question
for you."

Moments later, armed with the knowledge of
where the trouble spot was most likely to be and
with Sam's gunbelt and revolver on the seat beside
her, Deirdre raced toward Lodge Pole. Sally had told
her that the bar up the street from the one she had
taken her to was the place that the rougher elements
chose to hang out. If there was trouble, the older
woman had said, it was probably some of the new
cowhands she'd heard had been hired by the owner
of the Three Diamond Ranch to help with the spring
and summer work. Deirdre pushed the gas pedal to
the floor.

When Sam neared the Amigo Bar, he slowed Licorice to an ambling walk. Across the street, he saw
Andy, shotgun tucked in the crook of his arm. They
nodded to each other.

Outside the bar, Sam noted several mud-splattered
pickup trucks. One had the Three Diamond brand on
the side panel. Judging from the noise, nearly every
hand from the ranch was crammed into the Amigo.
It must have been a regular rebellion that had made
so many men leave the ranch on a Friday night.
Salters hadn't exactly told him what to expect, only
warning him that his boys were tired of taking the
long drive over the pass to get into Jackson, and that
Sam had better prepare to reinforce his authority if
he wanted Lodge Pole to stay quiet this summer. A
cold anger started to simmer inside him.

He dismounted, sliding off of Licorice's bare back and tossing the reins over the hitching rail that stood outside the bar. Andy appeared at his side.

"Follow me," Sam ordered. "But don't do anything unless I tell you. I'd like to handle this with as little fuss as possible. Let's see what the boys have in mind."

The interior of the bar was smoke-filled and noisy. And packed with cowboys and sleazy women. Sam didn't recognize a single female face, but he did know most of the men. He touched the brim of his hat and nodded to the nervous-looking bartender. "Evening, Bill," he said in a voice loud enough to carry over the racket. "How's it going?"

Bill had no chance to reply. Sam found his path obstructed by the lanky figure of Bud Henderson, the Diamond's foreman. There was a smug smile on the man's face.

"Well, if it ain't the chief," Henderson said in a sneering tone. "Our little party flushed you out after all. Took a while. Maybe you had to work up your nerve."

Sam narrowed his eyes. "Cut the crap, Henderson. What's all this for?" He gestured at the room. "You know I'm going to close this down for disturbing the public peace."

"Maybe." Henderson hitched his thumbs into his belt. The bar was almost silent now, and Sam could feel every eye on him. Henderson planned to challenge him! Unbelievable, since the last time he and the foreman had crossed, Henderson had been in the hospital for a week. But the man looked so sure of himself . . .

"Okay, folks," Sam declared. "This party's over. Anyone who wants just to have some fun, keeping it quiet enough not to disturb the rest of the town is welcome—"

"Want you to meet one of the new boys," Henderson interrupted him. He gestured toward a dark corner of the room, and Sam saw a giant of a man lumber out of the shadows. So *this* was the big surprise. The cold anger inside him grew. Some fools never learn, he thought.

"Henderson," he said, ignoring the hulk that was approaching. "You're dumber than those cattle you pretend to herd. Hell, you're dumber than a *sheep*," he added, using the highest insult that could be laid on a cowman. In the dim light, he could see high spots of color stain Henderson's cheeks. Sam turned to the assembled crowd.

"This is a civilized community," he said, his voice ringing in the stillness. "There are laws, and men to enforce them. I don't know how Henderson managed to bamboozle you people into thinking this was still the wild West, but I'm here to tell you that it is not! Lodge Pole is my home and the home of many other law-abiding, peaceful, *sensible* citizens. Anyone here who wants to fit into that category has my personal welcome to stay and have a good time within the limits of the town ordinances. Anyone who doesn't had better get!"

"Gonna hide behind your badge, Cassidy?" Henderson's words were mocking. The huge newcomer had reached his side and towered over the smaller man. " 'Cause Luke here ain't bothered by no *badge*." He spat the word.

Deirdre slipped inside the door of the bar in time to hear the last part of Sam's speech and to catch the lean cowboy's retort. No one seemed to notice her, and that didn't surprise her. The tableau made by Sam and the two men who confronted him was enough to hold any eye.

She saw with relief that Andy was there with his shotgun, but Sam's weapon was a heavy weight in her hand. What should she do? Or not do.

"I don't hide behind anything," Sam was saying. "I am the chief of police in this town, and if your friend Luke has any plans for me, they'd better be neighborly, because assaulting an officer with deliberate intent to harm is a felony."

"You're chicken," the lean man jeered. Deirdre sidled farther into the room, hiding the revolver under her jacket.

Sam gave a loud sigh. He put his hands on his hips and shook his head. "Andy . . ." he said casually, "you figure we have room in the cell for both these idiots, or is it gonna crowd the place up too much. Should I put the big one in the hospital?"

"Might be a good idea." Andy shifted the shotgun so that Deirdre could see he was covering the room. He saw her, but his expression warned her to make no move. Sam still hadn't noticed her, and she hoped he wouldn't. He needed all of his skill to handle this situation.

The giant started to move but stopped when Sam abruptly held up his hand. "Oh, by the way . . ." Sam said. "If this ends in a fracas, I promise every man-jack in this room that I'll investigate and prosecute anyone involved in planning it. There's a law against conspiracy, too."

A murmur ran around the room. Then one of the cowboys spoke up. He was a young man with sun-bleached blond hair. "You didn't tell us nothing about no trouble with the law, Bud," he said. "Just said Luke'd kick the chief's—"

"Shut up, Joe," the other man snarled. "He's just bluffing you."

"He's not doing any such thing." Deirdre used her voice in the way her father had taught her when she needed to command respect and authority. "It's a recognized law in every state in the union. In fact, I believe that the conspiracy aspect could land a number of you in a federal court."

"Who the hell are you?" the man called Bud yelled at her.

Sam barely resisted smashing his fist into the insulting face. Deirdre's presence made him unsure of his emotional control, but she had certainly captured the attention of everyone in the room. And he could see that she was holding his revolver. She had come here to help him!

"This *lady*," he said, "is Deirdre Wilcox, late of Washington, D.C., and the daughter of Senator Wilcox of Georgia. When she speaks of the law, I'd advise all of you to listen."

More murmurs. Then people began to rise and leave the bar.

My God, Sam thought. It worked. Between them, he and Deirdre had bluffed the crowd. He wasn't sure whether he should make her an official member of the force for this or to fire her again for disobedi-

ence. Then he remembered his own case of disobedi-
ence. She had acted *exactly* as he had, although with
less youthful bravado. He thought back to his claim
that they were such different people. Maybe he'd
been wrong.

Bud and his animal, Luke, were looking decidedly
unhappy. Henderson yelled curses at the departing
people, but it was plain that he had lost control,
and Sam imagined that both of the men would find
themselves looking for new jobs in the morning.

"Give it up, Henderson," he said quietly. "We
don't need any of this." He put his hand on the
man's elbow and started to lead him toward the door.

But Henderson exploded. Sam ducked his swing-
ing fist easily and was pulling his arm around behind
his back to immobilize him when he heard Deirdre
cry a warning. He released Henderson and barely
avoided the bear hug that Luke lunged at him.
Caught in those thick arms, Sam knew he'd end up
with a crushed rib cage at the very least. He whirled
around and faced Luke, crouching down in a fighting
stance designed to give him the greatest mobility. He
and Luke circled each other.

Deirdre sprang into action the moment she saw
that Sam had avoided the huge man's grasp. Andy
was covering the two combatants, so she ran over to
where the smaller man was recovering from the
sprawl that Sam had thrown him into on the floor.
She stepped on his neck and placed the barrel of the
revolver in his ear.

"I know how to use this, mister," she hissed.
"And if you move one millimeter, I will."

NINE

Sam feinted at Luke. The big man responded with another charge, easily avoided. Okay, Sam thought. This one never learned to think. He could probably take punishment clear into next week while he waited for a chance to crush his opponent against himself. Time for a little Oriental touch.

He moved to one side, luring the giant into another rush, but this time, he whirled and slammed the heel of his boot at the man's head, just behind the temple. Luke fell like a redwood tree. A spatter of applause filled the room.

Sam bent to make certain that he'd done no more than put the man to sleep and gave Andy orders to put the heavy manacles on him. "He'd probably snap handcuffs," he added. Then he saw Deirdre.

She was a sight! Dressed still in her prissy business suit and seductive blouse, she posed like an Amazon fighter over a fallen male foe, her foot on

Henderson's sun-darkened bare neck and his revolver *stuck barrel-end* in the man's ear. Sam didn't know whether to laugh or weep at the sight.

Since they still had an interested audience, including Bill, the bartender, he did neither, but went over to her and thanked her quietly for her help, taking the revolver gingerly from her. Then he cuffed Henderson and jerked the man to his feet.

"You're damn lucky I won," he said to the cringing man who was still regarding Deirdre with fear in his eyes. "Miss Wilcox is kind of fond of me, and you remember what the Indian women around here did to folks who hurt their men, don't you?" Beneath his tan, Henderson paled further.

"Chief Cassidy." It was the young blond cowboy who had earlier challenged Henderson. He had his hat in his hands and a contrite look on his face. "I think I can speak for all the rest of the boys when I say we learned our lesson here tonight. I promise, you won't have no more trouble from us."

"That's good to hear," Sam replied. "If it's okay with Bill here, you boys can stay and finish your partying. As long as—"

The cowboy grinned. "I know, sir. As long as we behave by the rules."

Deirdre trailed behind the two officers and their prisoners as they left the bar. Two of the cowboys had volunteered to help Andy with Luke, and suddenly she felt like an outsider in the situation. She hadn't been able to tell from Sam's expression or voice what his reaction to her presence and participation was, but she expected that she would face a repetition of the scene after the moose incident. He had told her to go home, and there was no denying that she had willfully disobeyed.

Instead of following the group to the station, she went over to where Licorice was tethered to the hitching rail. The mare nosed her, and Deirdre patted the velvety skin and scratched the warm, coarse-haired ears. Then, to her own horror, she felt tears fill her eyes and flood down her cheeks.

Sam could have been killed. The realization hit her like a blow.

She had to get out of sight! To be seen bawling like a child when she had just finished helping stand off two wild cowboys would be far too embarrassing to even contemplate. She gave Lic one more pat and fumbled for the keys to the Jeep.

Once home, she stripped quickly and put on her familiar, comforting nightgown. Then she crawled into the bed, wrapped herself in the sheet and a light blanket, and wept as freely and loudly as she needed.

Sam paused at the front door of Deirdre's house. The lights were all out, but the Jeep indicated that she was inside. And he could hear the strangest sounds faintly through the open window. He tried the door. It was unlocked. He let himself in.

He found her in the bedroom, all wrapped up and sobbing as if her heart was broken. Sam didn't say a word. He just took off his hat, belt, badge, and boots and climbed into the bed with her, drawing her into his embrace and murmuring words of comfort. He stayed, holding her, long after the sobbing had ceased and she was breathing easily in sleep.

*   *   *

Sunlight hit her face, waking Deirdre. She opened her eyes and winced at the pain their puffiness caused her. Memory of the events of the night before came back in a rush. All were clear except the dream of being held by Sam and hearing his words of consolation, praise, and even endearment. What a dream, she thought, sitting up and groaning at the headache that pounded in her temples. Her hysterics must have given way to hallucination, she decided, and she wondered if she ought to call her doctor back in Washington and report the episode. Certainly, her high-strung nerves had never given her *mental* problems before.

She stretched, feeling the tension in her back. That, she was sure, had been caused by bending over the cowboy and keeping him immobile until Sam and Andy had dealt with the other man. Then she got up and automatically started to make her bed. Her hand touched the pillow, and she froze.

Several strands of short black hair lay on the pillowcase beside her own long blond ones. Slowly, she picked them up and studied them. It had been no dream, she realized gradually. Last night, while she had been in the grip of her emotional maelstrom, Sam Cassidy had held her and brought her peace.

The sound of a vehicle pulling into her drive made her start. She dropped the hairs and stood, staring at the door as she heard the sound of boots on her steps and porch.

"Deirdre?" It was Sam. "You up yet?"

She glanced in the vanity mirror, grimacing at what she saw in the reflection, but told him to come in. He had seen her last night; he ought to be able to handle the results this morning. She grabbed a robe and went into the living room.

He gave her a smile. "You look like hell," he said, his tone kind in spite of his words. He dropped an armload of packages on the couch.

Deirdre ran a hand through her tangled hair. "I just now woke up," she confessed. "No chance to repair the damages."

"No need." He started to fuss with the packages. "I have the prescription for your recovery right here."

"Hunh?" She pressed her hand to her forehead. "What are you talking about?"

He held up a pair of strange-looking pants with boots attached. "These are waders," he explained. "You and I are taking the day off. We're going to go fishing, drive into Jackson, play tourist, have dinner, and just generally relax."

"Sam, I . . ."

He smiled, and his expression was full of tenderness. "This time, Deirdre, will you just do as I ask?"

Laughing, she agreed. While she showered and dressed in jeans and a shirt, Sam prepared them both breakfast. Once his powerful version of coffee entered her bloodstream, the headache and weakness vanished, and she felt like her old self again. While they ate, Sam explained that the county sheriff had picked up Luke and Bud Henderson, and that the two were incarcerated in the county jail, awaiting preliminary hearings on Monday. Andy would hold down the fort in Lodge Pole. When she finally worked up her nerve to ask his opinion of what she had done last night, he surprised her by reaching over and taking her hand.

"What you said and did took a lot of brains and guts, Deirdre. If it hadn't been for your help, someone might have been badly hurt. My only concern was your reaction afterward."

She flushed. "I came completely unglued, didn't I?"

"Honey, have you ever been in a violent situation like that before?" he asked, still holding her hand tightly.

"Never," she admitted. "I guess the moose was the closest. I've been involved with intellectual confrontations all my life. But that's different."

"Well, you kept your nerve for as long as necessary." He squeezed her hand. "Dammit, Deirdre. I was so *proud* of you."

Tears filled her eyes. "I didn't think, I just . . . did."

"I know." For a moment, Sam teetered on the brink of telling her what had happened to him in Los Angeles but decided that the further away they could stay from the subject of violence today, the better for her. She needed sunshine, fresh air, and recreation, and he intended to see that she got all. And on Monday, when he would have to return to Jackson for the hearing, she was also going to get a checkup by his doctor. He had already phoned George at his Jackson home to make the appointment.

She admitted to never having fly-fished before so he drove to a meadow just outside of town and taught her the rudiments of casting. She caught on quickly.

"It's a little like badminton or Ping-Pong," she

declared when the fly landed exactly where he had told her to cast. "You have to be precise and delicate or you'll overshoot."

"Not a bad comparison." Sam patted her shoulder. "Now let's go try the real thing."

The "real thing" Deirdre soon discovered was trickier. First, she had to figure out where the darned fish were. Then she had to wade into a fast-moving stream of icy waters that chilled her feet and legs even with the protective waders. But the sun was warm on her face and upper body so the discomfort was bearable. Her main problem was keeping her little lure from hanging up in cottonwoods that grew in abundance along the streambed. Several times, Sam goodnaturedly clambered up one of the trees to free her line.

"Don't be discouraged," he told her. "It takes practice to become accomplished at this." She assured him truthfully that she was having fun in spite of feeling clumsy.

"When I was a little girl," she said, "and my father was still just a state senator, my mother enrolled me in formal dance lessons. All preparations for the eventual and inevitable debutante ball. I hated it at first, felt all legs and feet and ankles. But after a while, I could waltz with the best of them."

"I bet you could." Sam felt mixed emotions at her little story. It was endearing to think of her as an awkward child, trying to ape grown-up gracefulness. But it also reminded him of the great gap between them socially. Oh, he could dance. When he had been young, there had been plenty of females willing to teach him that and much more. But dance *lessons* were not part of the son of an orange rancher's life. And he was fairly certain that Deirdre was the first woman he'd ever met who had actually had an old-fashioned society debut.

He studied her as she worked, tongue-tip nipped between white teeth, trying to get that fly into the shadow under the overhang where he was certain a trout lurked. He had known her for less than a week, but it seemed like months. He already felt the ache of loneliness that he now knew would come with her departure in the fall.

Suddenly she let out a shriek of delight, and he saw that her pole was bent almost double. "Reel it in," he yelled, splashing through the stream to stand at her side. "Keep the line taut!"

Deirdre felt laughter bubbling up in her. The thrill of hooking the fish was unlike anything she had experienced before. She followed Sam's excited instructions and soon the fish was thrashing in the water at her booted feet. Sam reached down and pulled it out.

"A beauty," he stated, regarding the fish proudly.

"Let him go." She reached for the fly and carefully unhooked it from the trout's mouth. Sam looked at her and then nodded. He bent over and carefully placed the fish back in the water. It scooted quickly away, heading back to its refuge beneath the bank.

"Will it be all right?" Deirdre stepped close to Sam and put her hand on his arm.

"A little sore for a day or so maybe," Sam reassured her. "But I'll lay you dollars to doughnuts that sometime when we need a meal, we can come back and catch him again."

"He was my first," she said solemnly. "I want him to live." Sam put his arm around her shoulders and hugged her gently.

"So be it," he declared. "Now the fishing lesson is over. Let's head for Jackson."

Deirdre's first view of the Grand Tetons took her breath away. Rising as they did like gigantic, snow-covered pyramids out of the valley floor, they seemed impossible geological phenomena.

"I've seen pictures," she said in an awed tone. "But I never thought the impact would be so staggering."

Sam chuckled. "They are something, aren't they. Wait until later in the summer when the valley's green and the hills are full of flowers. I can take you places you won't believe could exist on this earth. Makes it easy for a person to imagine what heaven's like."

They drove through the valley, and Deirdre absorbed the scenery like a sponge. It was beauty beyond anything she had ever known. Antelope grazed in the meadows, and when they neared the town, Sam pulled over so that she could see the herd of elk that wintered just outside of the resort.

"During the summer and autumn," he told her, "they roam up in the high meadows, but in the winter, they congregate here and the town provides winter feed to protect them from starvation."

"I love it!"

She felt the same way about Jackson. The resort was a mixture of western hype and touristy honky-tonk. The architecture was mostly log-cabin style with a maverick modern building here and there. The main part of the town circled a large, grassy park that sported entry gates made of twisted gray wood and elk skulls.

As they strolled the main shopping area, Sam explained that in a few weeks, the place would be jammed with visitors. Winter and summer, he said, the town drew skiers and sightseers by the thousands.

"I suppose it would be difficult to keep the kind of peace you favor in a place like this," she commented, giving him a teasing smile.

He returned the smile. "That's why I'm in Lodge Pole, Miss Analyst."

They bought sandwiches at a deli and sat in the park to have lunch. The air was warm, and they both shed their jackets.

Sam let his gaze linger on her while they ate. It was hard to remember that this beautiful, carefree, almost childishly delighted woman was the same person who had held a gun to the head of a man the night before and then had cried herself to sleep in his arms from the emotional backlash. Her eyes were clear and flashed a brighter blue than the sky. Her skin was . . .

"Oh, Lord," he said, jumping to his feet. "I forgot to warn you about the high-altitude sun." He held out his hand and helped her to her feet. "You're already sunburned."

Deirdre put a hand to her cheek. It did feel a bit warmer than usual. "It's all right," she said. "If I'm going to live here, I'd better get a protective base anyhow."

But Sam insisted on taking her to a drugstore and buying a tube of sunscreen. Then on to a western clothier for a cowboy hat. His concern for her complexion amused Deirdre, so she allowed him to pick out a wide-brimmed straw one. She set it on her head and mugged at her reflection in the mirror.

"Now I really do look native," she commented.

Sam felt something inside him twist at her words.

The rest of the afternoon, he took her to the better art galleries, introducing her to the owners and explaining her background. Deirdre felt as if she were a kid in a candy store. Most of the art was western-theme, and she knew of some dealers back in Washington who would pay top dollar for the works. An idea began to form in her mind.

She had a sizable trust fund left to her from her mother's estate. It would be easy for her to buy locally and sell at a profit to galleries she knew in the East. She could also act as an art broker, if a particular collector got hot for this style of painting and sculpture.

"I see wheels turning," Sam said when she made a side trip into a stationery shop and bought a small notebook. "Can I ask what's cooking in your fertile mind?"

Deirdre explained her idea to him. "If the market's as good as I think it will be, I could stand to make a considerable profit as a middleman."

He looked down at her with amazement showing in his eyes. "You never stop, do you. Always wheeling and dealing. Organizing and planning. You're supposed to be relaxing."

"I am." She gave him an impish grin, and he felt that strange twisting again. "I'm never more relaxed than when I'm on the scent of a good art deal."

By evening she had collected a long list of artists' names and addresses. Some works, she knew she would have to buy through the local galleries to keep from seeming to compete unfairly. But, she reasoned, business was business, and she could save the costs of gallery profits by going directly to the artists.

Sam finally called a halt to her traipsing in and out of shops, complaining that the sandwich had long since been disgested and he was starved. Deirdre, who was far too excited about her new idea to be moved by the thought of food, looked up at him and said teasingly, "I guess it must take a lot of fuel to keep a big, handsome body like that going."

Sam fought off the urge to take her into his arms right there on the sidewalk. She was so appealing with her straw hat, sunburned nose, and trim figure clad in jeans and a plaid shirt. Suddenly he realized that she had hooked him just like the trout she'd caught this morning. The question was, come fall would she release him to lurk alone in his solitude again?

"I know a great restaurant," he said, hearing a slight gruffness in his own voice. "In the high tourist season, you have to make reservations weeks in advance. We shouldn't have any trouble getting in now, though." His stomach was churning, and he told himself it was from hunger. But in his heart, he knew he was suffering from a far more serious craving. A craving for the impossible possibility that Deirdre wouldn't leave.

"Okay," she said, wondering at the sudden glum mood that seemed to come over him. "You're the boss. Lead on." Maybe, she decided, he was one of those people who get cranky when they're hungry. She had a friend back in Washington who was a monster in the morning unless she ate immediately upon rising. Remembering her friend made her think of returning home, and that made her think of leaving Sam. And suddenly she knew how badly that would hurt. She linked her arm with his, realizing that she had become very fond of him in just a short time. What was she going to feel like after months of close association?

Her touch surprised him, but Sam welcomed the warmth of her hand against his elbow. "I didn't think you liked anyone but yourself to be the boss," he said, looking down at her and feeling affection for her rising in him. "You may work for me, but I've got a feeling it's going to always be on your terms."

"Only if I believe I'm right and you're wrong," she replied, reminding him of how alike they were in that respect.

They were able to get a table immediately. The head waiter led them to a secluded corner, where they enjoyed a delicious meal. Sam put his worries about his emotions in the back of his mind and simply enjoyed Deirdre's company.

For her part, Deirdre was enjoying a sense of new-found freedom. In the part of the country where she had come from, they would have been turned away from a restaurant of this quality, dressed as casually as they were. Customs were different here, but refreshing.

Sam paid for the meal and was about to suggest that they stop at one of the more colorful bars for a beer before traveling home when he heard a voice call his name.

"Cassidy? Sergeant Sam Cassidy?"

Sam turned and saw his past come running up to reach for his hand.

_____ TEN _____

Deirdre watched, puzzled, as a small, balding man rushed up to Sam and began pumping his hand and acting as if he'd found a long-lost relative.

"You just dropped out of sight, Sergeant," he said. "Like you'd jumped off the end of the world. Nobody could get a line on you, and don't think we didn't try, man." He glanced at Deirdre. "Hey, is this your wife, Sarge? What'd you do? Come up here and get yourself a ranch and a pretty woman to go with it?"

Sam sighed inwardly. Tad Browning was one of the reporters who had championed his case, had built him up to be some sort of super-cop, had been seriously infected with hero worship, and he knew there was no way short of outright rudeness that he would be able to shake off the little man immediately. And he also knew that once Browning discovered that Deirdre knew nothing about the event, she would be treated to the reporter's golden-glow description of Sam's heroism.

"We were going to get a beer," Sam said. "If you're finished with your dinner, you're welcome to join us, Tad. Deirdre, this is Tad Browning. Tad, this is my *friend*, Deirdre Wilcox."

Deirdre shook the man's hand and saw that he was giving her a second look. But she was certain that she was unrecognizable as her old society self tonight.

But once the three of them were settled in a quiet section of one of the bars colorfully decorated to resemble an old-time saloon, and she discovered that Tad was a reporter, she began to wonder if he'd see through her disguise. As it turned out, however, she was of little interest to the man.

He explained to Sam that he was up in Jackson, doing a story for an upcoming issue of a travel magazine for his newspaper. Then he started in with the questions. What had made Sam leave Los Angeles? What was he doing here? Why hadn't he ridden out the departmental storm of jealousy?

"Hell, Sarge. You could have been *chief* if you'd stayed around," he said with vehemence.

Sam finally smiled. He ran a finger down the side of the beer glass. "Tad, I *am* chief. In a little burg called Lodge Pole on the other side of the pass. I have one officer, and Deirdre is my secretary and right hand. In fact, she helped me make an arrest last night."

"An arrest?" Tad's brown eyes gleamed interest. "Was it anything as spectacular as—?"

"Just a little local trouble." Sam took a sip of his beer.

Deirdre decided now was the time to take the plunge. "Tad, you keep referring to something that happened in Sam's past. I'm curious. Sam, would you mind?"

He looked resigned. "Believe about half of what you hear," he muttered.

"You mean you don't know?" Tad looked incredulous. When Deirdre shook her head, feeling that she wasn't actually lying, since she had only glimpsed the article, Tad launched into a detailed account of Sam's heroic actions. Deirdre noted that Sam seemed to grow more uncomfortable with each sentence. By the time the little reporter was through, Deirdre understood that the departmental policy had been to consider hostages as already dead people, and when Sam had taken it on himself to free them, bureaucracy had fallen on him like a stone wall.

"I call my own shots in Lodge Pole," he said when Tad had finally run out of steam. "Been there almost three years, and the town council has no problems with the way I handle things."

Deirdre bit her lip against the urge to tell the reporter about his nickname of Guardian Angel, but she knew that Sam had suffered enough embarrassment. Then Tad turned his attention back to her. "What's it like working as Sam's secretary, Miss Wilcox?"

"Interesting."

"How long—?"

"Deirdre's only been with me for a few days," Sam interrupted. "And she's only here for the summer. During the winter, we have so few people in the town that my officer and I can handle things ourselves.''

In a pig's eye, Deirdre thought. If that sty of a station was what he meant by "handling things." And she felt more than a little hurt that he was dismissing her so easily.

"You mean you aren't a native?" Tad asked.

Deirdre shook her head. "I'm from back East," she said evasively.

Sam pulled her out of the interrogation soup by announcing that they had a long drive across the pass to get home. Tad seemed reluctant to let them get away, but Sam skillfully extricated them and soon they were on the way back to Lodge Pole.

They drove in silence for a while. Then Deirdre felt compelled to tell Sam that she had seen his clippings. "I didn't really read them closely," she said. "I assumed they were personal to you, and as soon as I realized they had nothing to do with the running of the office, I put them back."

"And said nothing to me about them?" His tone was neutral.

"What could I have said?"

He laughed and covered her hand with his own. "For one thing, you could have thrown it into my face that you and I are cut from the same bolt of cloth in at least one way. When the chips are down, we act. We don't stand around with our faces hanging out, waiting for 'orders.' " He spoke the last word as if it were unclean.

"Now that you mention it . . ."

"Deirdre." He sounded serious. "No one in town

knows about it, and I'd really appreciate it if it could stay that way. It's bad enough that they hung that Angel nickname on me.''

"You'd better hope your reporter friend doesn't decide to add a feature on you to his little visit up here," she warned. "He thinks you're the finest thing since sliced bread, you know.''

Sam digested her words. She was right, and he should have thought of it himself. Sometimes the free press was a real pain. And Browning really seemed to have a screw loose.

"At least he didn't recognize you," he said. "I'll bet my socks that he'd have followed up on a Washington socialite working a one-horse police station.''

"Well, the horse is Licorice," she teased. "That gives it all the class it needs." Sam's laughter filled the car.

When they pulled up to her house, Deirdre was dozing, her head on Sam's shoulder. He woke her with a gentle kiss.

"Inside and to bed with you, sleepyhead," he said, caressing her hair. "Sleep in. It's been a busy day, and you don't have to come to work on Sunday.''

"But you do?"

He hesitated. "Part of the day I'll cover. But I do go to church in the morning. You wouldn't be interested in coming along, would you?''

Deirdre knew her expression registered surprise. "I'd like that very much, Sam. But you don't strike me as the religious type.''

He smiled and kissed her lightly. "I know very few people who've seen a gun aimed at them and then go off who've remained alive without some sense of a higher power being on their side."

"I think I understand." Deirdre slipped her arms around his neck. "What time?"

"I'll be by at ten-thirty." He kissed her lingeringly and then shooed her into her house with orders to sleep soundly. She did.

The next morning, she woke refreshed. After breakfast, she gave her father a call, filling him in on her idea about doing some art brokering. He seemed to approve of the plan. But when she mentioned her thoughts about staying past the end of the summer, he sounded concerned.

"Honey . . ." Richard Wilcox said in the rich southern voice that made him such a compelling orator, "we all agreed you needed some time off, but your natural home is here. Where all the moving and shaking is taking place."

Deirdre laughed. "You'd be amazed at the "moving and shaking' that goes on where you'd least expect it. Anyway, it's just a thought. I've hardly been here long enough to really make up my mind." And, she thought, she had only known Sam a week come tomorrow. She chatted with her father for a while longer and then told him she had to get ready for church.

"I'm glad to hear that," he said. "Did the minister come by and call on you?"

"Actually, no." Deirdre hesitated. "I'm going with my boss."

"The policeman?"

"The chief. He's a . . . very unusual man, Dad. I think you'd like him."

"I didn't care much for him firing you the first day on the job."

"There were extenuating circumstances. I'll write you a letter this week and tell you about them. Anyhow, I'm reinstated, so there's no problem."

"I have a hunch there's a lot going on I ought to know about." Richard Wilcox's tone was suspicious. "But you are a grown-up woman now, and I suppose I know better than to meddle in your business." When they finally said good-bye, Deirdre smiled to herself. Her father could no more stop meddling in her life than he could stop breathing. But it was a loving meddling so she really didn't mind.

She dressed simply but elegantly, wearing a tailored silk dress and fixing her hair up in a twist the way she had worn it when she had first met Sam. She applied makeup with a light touch. She had just finished when she heard the sound of his Jeep in her driveway.

When she opened the door at his knock, she gasped in surprise. An entirely new Sam Cassidy stood before her.

He was hatless, his black hair neatly combed, and he wore a fashionably cut gray suit that would have been very much in place on the streets of Washington.

"You look beautiful," he said, taking her hand and kissing her on the cheek.

"So . . . so do you."

He grinned. "The threads surprise you? I keep up, Deirdre. My wardrobe isn't all uniforms and jeans, although they make up the major part. I do travel to Denver now and again."

As he drove her to the small community church that served the citizens of Lodge Pole, Sam reflected that this summer he wouldn't be making any trips in search of casual romance. The woman beside him was far too compelling to leave even for a day. Later, after she was gone for good, he might take some time to try and forget her with other women, but deep inside, he knew it wouldn't work well.

During the service, Deirdre found herself much more aware of Sam than of what was happening liturgically. He responded with a reverence that amazed her, considering the earthiness of his nature. He had not, she realized, been kidding her about his spiritual feelings.

Many of the people she had already met in Lodge Pole were in the congregation. Sally, her granddaughter, and a middle-aged couple she assumed were Julie's parents. The Edwardses were there, and a number of the people she had met while waitressing during the last week. No one seemed unduly surprised at her presence with Sam, and she felt quite comfortable. She and her father attended services regularly so, she reflected, she was merely repeating an old habit in a new locale.

Afterward, Sam introduced her to the minister and to a number of other people, but she could sense that he was in a hurry to leave. Andy, she remembered, had been on solitary duty for almost twenty-four hours.

"Go on," she told him. "I can catch a ride with someone else or walk. It wasn't far."

Sam eyed her high heels. "It'll seem far in those stilts." He called out to John Edwards, asking if he could give her a lift since he needed to get back on duty and relieve Andy.

"We can do better than that," Martha Edwards, a short, plump woman with graying auburn hair, declared. "Miss Wilcox, won't you please come have Sunday dinner with us. John and Tommy have told me so much about you, and I want a chance to find out just how much the rascals have been lying to me." Deirdre accepted with pleasure, and Sam slipped away after promising to call her that night.

The Edwards's Sunday dinner, it turned out, was far more of a social event than Deirdre expected. Apparently preparing a large meal for a number of churchgoers, including the minister, was a regular practice of Martha's. As Deirdre helped in the kitchen, listening to the women chat and occasionally answering a question directed at herself, she was reminded of similar gatherings at her Georgia home when her mother had still been alive and plenty of family lived nearby. Nostalgia washed through her, and she felt her eyes mist.

Martha Edwards was standing close enough to notice. Quietly, she asked if Deirdre were all right.

Deirdre blinked back the tears. "I was just remembering," she replied. "Suddenly all this reminded me of when I was a little girl and life was much, much simpler."

Martha patted her arm. "Maybe you've come back home. In the spiritual sense, that is."

Deirdre dwelt on those words for the rest of the afternoon.

Tommy insisted on the honor of driving her home, and she took advantage of the opportunity by having the youth show her some of the winter-rental homes. She could hardly infringe on Senator Thorton's hospitality through the months when she knew he and his family used their house fairly frequently. If she actually did decide to stay in Lodge Pole for a while longer, she'd have to find another place. Several of the homes Tommy pointed out looked like good possibilities, and she made a note to get in touch with their owners once she made up her mind.

Back in the Thorton home, she busied herself with laundry and housekeeping tasks that she had neglected over the hectic, event-filled week. And she had come here to *rest*, she thought wryly.

Dinner was a sandwich. After the feast of the meal Martha had prepared, Deirdre doubted that she would be hungry for the rest of the week. She then curled up in a chair to read a novel.

Sam tapped his fingers impatiently on the desk as he listened to the phone ring. Eight . . . nine . . .

"Hello?" Deirdre's voice sounded fuzzy, as if she had been sleeping. Sam glanced at his watch.

"I didn't wake you, did I?" he asked. "It's only nine."

"I fell asleep in the chair," she confessed. "I was reading, but I guess the story wasn't engrossing enough."

"Or you were overly tired." He tried to inject the proper amount of sternness into his voice. "I want you to go on to bed as soon as I hang up."

"Oh, of course, Master." The words dripped sarcasm.

"Deirdre . . . I worry about you." Sam gripped the receiver.

"Why?"

He swallowed hard. "Because, dammit, woman, I *like* you. Now listen to me. In the morning we're going back to Jackson. I have to show up at the preliminary, and you have an appointment to see my doctor, George Bennett."

"What! Just where do you get off making *doctor* appointments for me? You are not my keeper!"

"Calm down!" Sam closed his eyes. He had shouted the words. Taking a deep breath, he repeated them softly. "Deirdre, doesn't it make sense to at least get acquainted with the man? You are out here for your health, after all. And this last week would stress a saint."

There was a moment of silence on the line. Then he heard her agreeing that he was right. Relief flooded him.

Deirdre hung up the phone, wondering at what she had just heard. Sam Cassidy had said that he liked her. What exactly did that mean in his language? And he had gone to the personal trouble of making a doctor appointment for her. She wasn't sure whether to think of the gesture as high-handed or . . . caring.

As she prepared for bed, she examined her own feelings for him. In one week, he had infuriated her, humiliated her, caressed her, kissed her into passionate insanity, caused her to respect and admire him.

Even to like him. Was she subconsciously considering staying on because of him?

That would be idiotic. All right. He was handsome and usually, lately, likable. But to plan the future on the basis of her relationship with Sam was utter nonsense. In fact, if she was really thinking that way underneath it all, she'd be far better off leaving *now*. She knew that she had never really been in love, in spite of the affair with that snake-in-the-grass back in Washington. She had no picture of herself as bound to a man by unbreakable ties of emotion. And from what he had said, Sam felt the same way about women. Maybe they would become lovers, but Deirdre believed firmly that she could keep part of herself free and able to fly whenever she wanted.

Sam picked her up the next day, but he seemed moody, and since she felt the same way, she turned on the radio so that they could remain silent without feeling awkward. The scenery still awed her, but she made no verbal comment on it. Once in town, Sam dropped her off at the professional building housing the doctor's office. He would be back, he told her, as soon as possible. He didn't think the preliminary would take very long.

She found George Bennett to be a likable man, easy to talk to. She explained her medical history and had him laughing when she described how the first week of her "rest cure" had gone.

"It's your life, Miss Wilcox," he said finally. "You have to teach yourself how to slow down. I think removal from your old environment was a very good idea, and I also think you might consider staying away for longer than just three months. You've had years and years to learn to be an overachiever. It'll take some time to learn a more passive routine.''

Deirdre smiled. ''I had been giving the idea some thought.''

Dr. Bennett gave her a routine physical and ran a few tests, just for his records, he told her. She checked out, and he released her with the reminder to make herself slow down when she found life moving too fast.

She waited nearly two hours for Sam, thankful that she had brought along the novel that had put her to sleep the night before. When he finally appeared, he was like a thunderstorm entering the room.

He said nothing, but gestured curtly for her to come. He looked more angry than she had ever seen him appear, and fury seemed to roll from him in tangible waves. When they reached the Jeep, he handed her the keys.

''You'd better drive,'' he said. ''In my state of mind, I'm liable to have an accident and kill us both.'' Then he slammed himself into the passenger seat.

Wordlessly, Deirdre started the Jeep. Clearly, things had not gone well at court, but she would wait, she decided, until Sam was ready to talk about it. She drove to a fast food place since it was past noon, and she was hungry. When she asked, Sam declared he was too mad to eat.

They were all the way over the pass before he spoke. ''Pull off to the side, Deirdre. None of this is your fault, and you shouldn't have to suffer from my bad temper. I apologize.''

"Accepted, of course."

He looked at her and gave her a smile. "How did things go with Bennett?"

"Clean bill. As long as I keep a rein on myself."

His smile faded. "I could use some of that advice, too. Deirdre, the judge let those two skunks off. Old man Salters hired himself a fancy lawyer, and the bastard sweet-talked the judge into believing that they were just good old boys blowing off some steam! I barely avoided a contempt charge because I lost my cool and forgot my courtroom manners. If I catch either of them in my town, I'm liable to put aside my badge and get really barbaric!"

ELEVEN

Deirdre felt a wave of indignation rising in her. "How could it happen? They commited a *crime*."

Sam leaned his head back on the seat and shut his eyes as if against some inner pain. "Unfortunately, like all human institutions, the law has flaws. The lawyer and Salters had those two bums all slicked up and dressed in *business* suits. Where they got one to fit that gorilla, I'll never know. The judge was in a good mood—must have had a nice weekend. The prosecutor mishandled a point or two, and the hired defense made a big point that I was a relative new-comer to the area, liable to overreact to the 'playful-ness' of local ranch workers. The case was flushed in the first five minutes."

She unbuckled her seat belt and slid over next to him. Stroking his hair, she said, "But it wasn't your fault, so why take it so hard? Maybe they learned their lesson and won't give you any more trouble."

He opened his eyes, and she could see years of accumulated cynicism in the green depths. "Henderson was born making trouble," he said. "The only reason I figure Salters saved his butt was because he does know how to keep his men in line. This time of the year, Salters wouldn't want to have to be breaking in a new foreman. I should have realized that."

Deirdre put her arms around his neck. "I thought my dad had chosen a hard life by going into politics. But I think you've picked a more difficult one." She laid her head on his shoulder.

Sam unfastened his own seat belt and put his arms around her, letting her warmth and sweetness replace all the anger and bitterness he had been feeling. Just sitting here with her, close like this, it seemed nothing in the world could hold him down for long. *Deirdre,* he thought, feelings swelling inside of him. *How empty life will be when you're gone.*

For the next few weeks Deirdre found that she had settled into a comfortable and pleasant life. Her work at the station kept her close to Sam, and whenever he could, he spent time with her off hours. They had lunch and dinner together, sometimes at one of their houses, sometimes at Sally's. The townspeople accepted them as a courting couple, to judge from the teasing and friendly jibes, but Deirdre wondered if that was really true. When they were alone and away from the station, Sam and she indulged in considerable physical attention to each other, kissing and caressing but never going beyond the point of no return. Some reluctance to total physical commitment seemed to hold each of them back from too much seduction. Their friendship grew; certainly, she knew on her part. Oh, there were times when she wanted to wring the big man's neck for some mess he left on his desk when she was away, and they got into frequent arguments over her filing system, which she defended as logical and he denounced as impossible, but she considered this a normal part of a working relationship, not a threat to what was growing between them. Away from work, she discovered that in addition to their romantic episodes, she could *play* with Sam Cassidy. They went riding, she mounted on a gentle mare borrowed from Sally, and he showed her the wonders of the mountains in early summer. Vistas of meadows filled with blue, white, yellow, lavender; and scarlet wildflowers; moose— from a safe distance—munching the sweet grass next to the streams swelled by melting snows in the highland; beavers busily rebuilding damage done to their dens during the long winter and already beginning to gather foodstuffs for the next cold season. Deirdre was enchanted with it all.

Sam was enchanted with Deirdre. She still maintained that queenly dignity that had both galled him and attracted him when he had first seen her. She could handle every situation that had arisen in the course of her duties with quiet competence. Once, when he had arrested a tourist who had sped through town as if he were on the open road, she had spoken a few soft words to the outraged man and he had quit sputtering and cursing and had paid his fine without further fuss.

And he could tell that the townspeople liked having her in the station. Several had commented that they felt an extra sense of security because she was available to relay messages to the two officers. And they liked her stylishness.

But, Sam had noted, she wore the local uniform of jeans and a shirt when she wasn't involved in work or some other dress-up occasion. She had almost become a chameleon—the executive secretary at work, but the ordinary woman of Lodge Pole the rest of the time. Not that with her looks she could ever be ordinary, of course.

Reluctantly, he began to realize that the hook he had felt in his heart when they had made the first trip into Jackson had been transformed into silken webs that were drawing him ever closer to her. One morning late in June, he arrived very early at the station, sending a sleepy and grateful Andy home. He sat at his desk and began to write out a résumé. Then he took out a recent issue of a law-enforcement magazine and studied the want ads, looking for a position somewhere near the Washington area. He hated the thought of leaving Lodge Pole, but he suspected that he would hate being parted from Deirdre more. For the first time in his life, Sam Cassidy believed he was falling in love.

When she arrived a few hours later, greeting him cheerily and settling down immediately to type up Andy's report for the night shift, he felt sure of it. Breaking their rule against office intimacies, he gave her a kiss on the soft skin just below her ear before going out to walk the streets.

After he left, Deirdre touched the place his lips had caressed. What was that all about, she wondered.

e had actually seemed a little gruff when she had first come in. Then the kiss. Strange.

She finished Andy's few paragraphs quickly and filed them. When she turned, she noticed some writing on Sam's desk and picked up the paper, wondering if he wanted it typed. But when she began to decipher his scrawl, amazement filled her. Why was he making a résumé? The only reason she could think of was that he was planning to look for a new job. Then she saw the magazine and the circles drawn around several want ads.

"Oh, my God," she whispered. The circles were all for jobs in the area of her old hometown.

Sam's emotions grew stormier and stormier as he walked the familiar streets of Lodge Pole. How could he even consider leaving this place? His commitment here was for a lifetime, and he had only known Deirdre less than a month. If only she could be content to live here. . . . But that was a crazy thought. He was chasing rainbows in his mind. To do that, she would have to feel the kind of love he knew his mother had for his father, and while they were certainly getting along, she had given him no indication that she felt anything more than a friendly infatuation. That was hardly love.

He felt helpless. There was no way to win. He walked on, hardly aware of where he was going until he found himself just outside the Amigo Bar and staring at the lean figure of Bud Henderson. Sam fought and achieved control over the rage that threatened to engulf him and then was shocked when Henderson seemed to give him a friendly grin.

"Morning, Chief," he said. "Been talking to an old buddy of yours." He jerked his head toward the interior of the bar. "Told him you'd be up this way 'bout now. Told him the town could set its watches by you."

"Sarge . . . Sam!" Tad Browning emerged from the dim interior, camera in hand. Before Sam could say a word, Browning had fired off several snaps of him. Sam raised a hand in protest.

Just then, Sam's walkie-talkie crackled. "One," he heard Deirdre's voice call. Just what he needed!

"What is it?" he asked, his tone brusque. No immediate answer. "Deirdre, what's the matter?"

"You sound busy." Her tone was tinny and cool. "It'll keep." Then she rung off, and he couldn't raise her with several presses of his call button.

"Trouble with your lady friend?" Henderson's voice was lightly mocking, and Sam caught himself just in time to keep from making a threatening retort in front of the reporter. Because of Tad Browning's presence, Henderson had him between a rock and a hard place, and his simmering emotional state concerning Deirdre wasn't helping.

"That was my *secretary*," he said. "Tad, what are you doing here?"

"Well," the small man said, smiling. "After I returned with the story on Jackson, I told my editor about meeting you, and he wants to run a follow-up. You know, a 'how Sergeant Cassidy fared after leaving the city.' "

Sam swore silently. The last thing he wanted was any more publicity. *Anywhere.* "And what are you doing here?" He turned to Henderson, hoping the man could read the unspoken message of warning in his eyes.

Henderson shrugged. "Supplies." He indicated the loaded pickup. "I stopped for a little refreshment, and met this newspaper fella talking to Bill. Seemed interested in Lodge Pole's Guardian Angel, so I told him what I knew."

"Yes." Tad sounded eager. "This young man told me how you had set an example for him to quit leading a wild life and to settle down and behave as an exemplary citizen."

"Did he now?" Sam narrowed his eyes. "Well, Tad, I hope you're still newspaperman enough to check out all of your sources."

Henderson started, anger in his pale-blue eyes. "You callin' me a liar, Cassidy?" Browning looked upset, too.

"I'm calling you a fool if you even spit on the sidewalk," Sam said. "Tad, I had this man in court on assault charges just a few weeks ago. His lawyer got him off, but he's bad news, and my advice to you is to check out everything he told you." Then he turned and strode up the street, ignoring the babble of curses and questions that the two other men flung at his back.

Deirdre paced the office, wondering what she should do. He had sounded so abrupt on the microphone that she knew he was involved in some police business and didn't need her to bother him.

But apparently she was bothering him. Otherwise, why the things on his desk? Had he unconsciously left them there for her to find, or was he just in such emotional turmoil that he actually forgot them? She hit her fist against her palm, impatient to have it out with him. They had agreed weeks ago to be honest with each other, and she believed that applied to their personal relationship as well as professional.

But when Sam walked in the door, a scowl on his face, she almost lost her nerve. "What's the matter?" she asked.

"You go first." He took off his hat and placed it on the rack. "You called me." He sat on the corner of his desk.

Seeing his expression, she started to laugh nervously. "You hardly look like you're in the mood for the sort of discussion I had in mind. Perhaps we should put it—"

"Bud Henderson is in town. He was talking to Tad Browning." Sam crossed his arms over his chest. "Does that give you a hint why I'm in a foul mood?"

"What's Tad Browning . . .?"

Sam rose and waved his arms around, causing her to retreat a few steps. When he expanded like that, he seemed to fill the entire room. "Browning's editor wants him to do another story on me, Deirdre," he explained. "A human-interest piece of junk, and Henderson was feeding him a line of crap so long—"

"I get the picture." She raised her hands. "Let me field for you. I've done it often enough for my father, and I should have no trouble—"

"I don't want you dragged into it." He sat and was frowning again. Browning worried him. Once he had been a hero to the man.

"Why not?"

"Because . . . because I don't." Hero images could change.

Deirdre walked around him and picked up the magazine and hand-written résumé. Wordlessly, she shoved them at him.

Sam felt suddenly dizzy. He was certain he had put them away in his desk, and he knew she didn't mess in his personal storage spaces. They were still disorganized. Proof that she had respected his privacy. So that meant he must have left them out in the open, where she considered everything fair game.

"I . . . I was just thinking," he lied, unable to meet her gaze. "I got here early and was just—"

"Sam." She put the papers down, and her voice was soft. "How do you feel about me? Honestly?"

He studied the floor. "I never had any trouble with this when I was sweet-talking a lie," he admitted.

"Sam, were you thinking of leaving here because of *me*?"

He nodded, still not looking at her. "You've become very important to me, Deirdre. So important that I can't stand the idea of your leaving."

"I don't think I'm going to." She smiled and walked back to stand in front of him.

Sam looked up. "What?"

She put her hands on his thighs, feeling the iron-hard muscles beneath the cloth. "I like it here. I like the people. I like the scenery. I believe I can be active in the art scene over in Jackson. I don't think the two of you klutzes can run this place efficiently even during the slow season, and most of all, Sam, I won't leave until I know if we really do have something important developing between us."

The words were barely out of her mouth before she was captured by his legs and her face was held gently between his palms. His lips covered hers, and Sam told her with his kiss that as far as *he* was concerned, that something was very important.

As she relaxed into it, yielding to his loving touch, Deirdre realized that there was a difference now. She pressed her body to his, enjoying the sense of security that his closeness always brought her and feeling the slow beat of passion starting at her core. But there was more . . .

Sam tangled his hands in her hair. For a change, she had worn it loose this morning, and he imagined the golden strands capturing his fingers and holding him prisoner forever, melded with her. A rush of emotion filled him, and he slid off the desk, pulling her tightly against him. He lost all sense of place and time and only wanted to become one with her.

Deirdre held on to his neck to keep from falling in the highly unlikely case that his arms would let her go. All of her muscles had weakened to a jelly stage, and she knew she would collapse in a helpless heap at his feet if he released her.

But she knew he wasn't going to let go. Now that they had both openly admitted their feelings and plans, she sensed that nothing short of a cataclysmic event would force him to free her. For a fraction of a moment, she wondered if she should have revealed so much so soon, but Sam's warm lips and words of endearment—words she had dreamed she had heard the night of the fight at the Amigo—convinced her that she had done right by confronting him. Sam needed a bit of prodding to open up his feelings.

But once they were opened . . .!

"You know . . ." he whispered, his lips against her throat, "I'm fool enough to want you here and now. Right here on this old desk you so tidily cleaned for me."

She laughed, running her fingers through his thick hair. "Wouldn't that be wonderful if someone walked in? We might even make the cover of one of those tabloids."

Her words made him laugh and brought him back a fraction closer to earth. He was still in the clouds, knowing that she had *chosen* to stay—and at least in part because of him. Given the rope of more time, no telling how far he could pull her into his life. Still chuckling, he moved down to kiss her breasts through the material of her blouse, pleased when he found the nipples already hard and peaked.

"Okay," he murmured. "No fooling around on the town's property." He straightened and loosened his embrace, taking her small chin in his hand. "But my home's my own, and Andy's on nights for the whole week. How about dinner at my place, and then we'll see what happens after that."

Deirdre gazed up into his eyes and knew what would happen. A leftover warning from her southern upbringing whispered at her that one did not make love to a man who hadn't declared intentions of marriage. But this wasn't the South, nor was she a virginal child anymore. And Sam was a man not measurable by the social yardsticks she had been raised with. Sam was a world all to himself.

"Sam . . ." she said, suddenly worried about *his*

reputation. "If we . . . I mean when we . . . You are the chief of police. Won't people talk?"

He laughed. "Honey, I think folks have figured we've been lovers since that fracas with Henderson and then me staying with you most of the night. And you haven't noticed either of us being shunned in church or *any* place, have you?"

"No." As a matter of fact, she had to admit that the townspeople had grown friendlier by the day, and that not one single person had made any kind of disparaging remark to her about her relationship with the Angel.

"So . . ." He chucked her chin lightly. "Will you come to dinner?"

She felt a mixed frisson of excitement and panic. Talk was easy for her, but if she went to him tonight, then she would be bound to follow through with her tentative plans to stay in Lodge Pole. It wouldn't be fair or honorable otherwise, and if there was one thing her father had taught her, fairness and honor paid off. Then she looked directly into Sam's eyes. "What time?" she asked.

He didn't answer. Just drew her in for a kiss so passionate that it left her breathless. They clung in an embrace so close that she felt as if her body melted into his hardness.

Another kiss. One that made the world spin, and then there was a sudden crashing sound and a flash of light. She felt herself pushed behind Sam's big body, but looking past his shoulder, she could see a gleeful Tad Browning, camera in hand in the doorway. Out on the sidewalk, a look of sardonic triumph on his lean face, was the Henderson man.

"A senator's daughter!" Tad chortled. "Sam Cassidy, I'm going to do a story on you that'll make you a national hero and hearthrob!" His face took on a slightly manic expression. "And I'm going to do it whether you like it or not."

TWELVE

Sam actually counted to ten. It was a fast count, but he did it nevertheless. And when he spoke, he tried his best to keep his tone quiet.

"Tad," he said, "if I didn't know that you were a responsible man at heart, you'd be in a great deal of pain right now because that camera would be—"

"Mr. Browning." Deirdre came around from behind the protection of his back. "I don't think Sam wants to be a national anything. In fact, I think you'd probably better give him that roll of film. Preferably as quickly as possible."

Tad Browning's face turned slightly red. "I'll do no such thing, Miss Wilcox. There still is freedom of the press in this country, you know." He clutched his camera to his chest.

"There's also invasion of privacy." Sam's voice had a dangerous edge to it.

Browning started backing out of the office. He

shook his head. "You're both public figures, and this station is a public building. If I had caught you at your home, that might have been different. Here, you were both fair game."

Sam surged forward, but Deirdre stopped him. "He's right," she said softly. "There's nothing we can do."

"I can appeal to your sense of honor!" Sam shouted at the retreating newsman. He felt angry and betrayed. And worse. He felt that the loveliness between himself and Deirdre had been dirtied by the little man with the camera and the power to splash their privacy in front of the public eye.

"My first duty is to the news!" The reporter ran out of sight.

Bud Henderson, who had been watching silently, threw the toothpick he had been chewing down on the sidewalk. "Gonna look mighty pretty in the newspapers, Miss Wilcox," he said, giving her a look that made her want to shudder. "Too bad the little guy couldn't have got you when you had that gun on me."

"Henderson . . .!" Sam's voice cut like a whip. He pointed to the toothpick. "Littering."

Slowly, insolently, the lean cowboy bent over and picked up the offending item. Then he touched the brim of his hat and winked. "Be seein' you two," he drawled, and ambled away in the direction Browning had fled.

Deirdre put her hands on Sam's arm. He was actually quivering with rage. "Go sit down," she told him gently. As he moved to do so, she shut the door.

"This changes nothing," she said, turning back to

look at him. He sat with his face in his hands. "I don't even think he'll be able to sell the picture. You may be human interest news back in Los Angeles, but you and I are news only to each other. I'm willing to bet that his editor won't run it."

"I feel like I've . . . dishonored you." He looked at her, misery in his eyes.

Deirdre walked over to stand behind him and rubbed the tight muscles of his back. "Wasn't that your plan for this evening?" she asked teasingly.

Sam slammed a palm down on the desk. "You aren't taking this seriously?"

"No. I'm not." She leaned over and kissed him. "I told you once before that I was used to newspeople poking into my business." Actually, she thought, she was more alarmed at the venom she had seen in Henderson's eyes, but she didn't mention it. Sam was upset enough.

"So, you think I'm overreacting?" He sounded calmer.

"You trusted Tad Browning. You have a right to be mad. But it's hardly the end of the world, and certainly has nothing further to do with us." She moved over to her own desk, giving him a sultry look as she sat. "We'll just have to confine affection to private places."

Later, however, alone in her house, preparing for Sam to come by and pick her up, Deirdre found that much of her bravado had slipped. Nervously, she chose the sexiest underwear, feeling somehow that she was doing something wrong. She cared for Sam, but would she ultimately be causing him more grief by becoming his lover when she wasn't totally committed to life in Lodge Pole. An extension of her recuperation period, yes. But for how long could she live away from the life she had grown up with.

Oh, for heaven's sake, she scolded herself, regarding her image in the mirror. *What you really grew up with before Dad moved to Washington was not so very different from Lodge Pole.*

One difference, however, she reminded herself as she slipped on a seductively silky cocktail dress, was that an unmarried lady and an unmarried man did not make an agreement to meet at the gentleman's home for dinner and lovemaking. At least she didn't *think* they did back then. Maybe she was naive.

But times have changed, she told herself. *Sam's a big boy, and you're a big girl.* Of course there was the chance that one or both of them would eventually be hurt emotionally, but it seemed they were both willing to take the gamble. She glanced at her watch.

Sam was late. That was unusual. She sprayed on an extra misting of cologne, and then moved around the house straightening things that were already in place.

Twenty minutes later, she debated calling him. But that really went against her grain. She started to feel angry. If some police business had come up, couldn't he have taken the time to call? Or given a message to someone else?

An hour later, she was furious. She undressed and put on jeans and an old sweater. A search of her refrigerator revealed that she was very low on groceries, so she decided to walk to the Edwards store and pick up a few things. If Sam came by while she was gone, too bad.

She was partway to the store when she heard a horn honking at her. Turning, she saw Sally driving her old beat-up Bronco and waving at her frantically. Puzzled, Deirdre went over to the car.

"Get in!" Sally opened the passenger door. "Sam's been shot!"

Deirdre felt her muscles turn to stone. She stared at Sally, unable to comprehend what she had just heard.

"Dee, didn't you hear me?" The older woman reached out and literally dragged her into the car. Suddenly, all of Deirdre emotions came to life.

"Is he . . . ? How badly is he . . . ?" Tears flooded her eyes, and her heart hurt so badly that she thought she would faint with the pain. She loved him! Now she knew. Now that it might be too late.

"He was bushwhacked," Sally said grimly, flooring the gas pedal and sending Deirdre slamming back against the worn seat. "Some skunk drove past his place just as he was fixing to get in his Jeep and fired a shotgun . . ."

"Oh, my God." Deirdre's world spun. He was dead! A shotgun!

Then, to her amazement, Sally started to chuckle. "Settle down, Dee," she said. "Sam ain't dead. Take a lot more'n lousy aim from a shotgun to finish that one off, let me tell you."

"Tell me!" Deirdre grabbed Sally's shoulder. "What *happened*?"

"Don't know all the particulars." Sally turned down a side street. "But Sam seen 'em coming and dove under the Jeep. Caught the shot mostly in his legs, and his boots protected a lot of him."

"Where is he?"

"At the doc's. Getting the shot picked out and cussing like a crazed rattler. Sent me to tell you, but I knew you'd want to come hold his hand. From what I heard, the operation's kinda painful."

"I didn't know there was a doctor in Lodge Pole." This part of town was unfamiliar to Deirdre.

"Ain't. Not a real one, anyhow." Sally pulled into a wide driveway in front of a rectangular building. Deirdre could hear the sound of several dogs barking. "Doc Turner's a vet," Sally explained. "The paramedic's gone for the week."

A few minutes later, Deirdre sat on a stool in front of a stainless-steel operating table from which both ends of Sam Cassidy dangled. One end was alternately swearing at the rotund, patient man working on his sheet-shrouded other end and between curses explaining to Deirdre what had happened.

"I didn't see who it was," he said, gripping her hands tightly. "Didn't recognize the truck. They ripped past about eighty, which was why I heard in time to know something was going down. I just instinctively dropped and crawled under the front of the Jeep."

"But not quite in enough time," Doc Turner muttered, dropping another pellet in a metal dish with a clink.

"Do you suppose it was . . ." Deirdre began, thinking of Henderson's malevolence. Sam cut her off.

"Andy has all the facts in the case. A few of the county deputies are helping him look for the truck. Highway Patrol's been informed, too. Ouch!"

"Can't you anesthetize him?" Deirdre begged the doctor. Sweat was beading Sam's face, and she knew he really was suffering.

Doc Turner shook his head. "I'm not trained or licensed to medicate humans, Miss Wilcox." He gestured at a bottle of bourbon sitting on a shelf. "Give him a healthy slug of that. Best I can offer."

"Fortunately," Sam muttered, "I'm up on my tetanus shots, otherwise, I'd have to ride into Jackson on my belly."

Deirdre couldn't help it. She started laughing, and when she realized that she was on the fringes of hysteria, she got up and took down the bottle, pouring a drink for herself as well as for Sam.

"How incapacitated will he be?" she finally managed to ask the vet. "And should I arrange to take him to see Dr. Bennett tomorrow?"

Doc Turner said he didn't think it would be necessary. "Just keep an eye on the wounds. If any infection starts to show up, then you ought to, but I think he'll be fine in a few days. Whoever did this used birdshot, and it didn't penetrate very deep."

"Deep enough," Sam groaned.

Deirdre insisted on taking him to her home. With Sally's help, she collected pajamas from his house, arranged for Tommy to take care of Licorice, and even brought the fixing for the meal he had planned to make for her to her own kitchen. Doc Turner had recommended a nonprescription ointment to be applied to the wounds on his legs, and she got a tube of it just as the pharmacy was closing for the evening. The druggist expressed concern and sympathy and told her to call him if she had problems or questions.

When they were finally alone, she knelt on the floor by the bed and put her arms around him. "I thought you were dead," she told him. "And I felt like I had died, too." Tears stung her eyes.

Sam raised up on his elbows, wincing as he did. "Honey, *nothing* could kill me before I made you mine." He hooked his arm around her neck and pulled her to him for a long, loving kiss.

"Then I'm afraid you're going to have to make a great effort to stay alive for a while longer," she said when he released her. "It's obviously out of the question for now."

"Think so?" There was a decided gleam in his eyes.

While she prepared dinner, he lay on the floor on a blanket, insisting that he could walk short distances, that to be immobile would make the wounds stiffen, and he wanted to be close to her. They discussed possible suspects, and while she learned that Bud Henderson headed his list, he had also included Tad Browning.

"I think the man's unstable," he explained. "He went way overboard to make a hero out of me before. Now that he knows I'm mad at him, maybe he wanted some kind of revenge. Then there's Luke, old man Salters . . ." He went on to list several more men in the area who could have grudges against him.

Deirdre raised an eyebrow. "No female possibilities? No scorned past loves. Whoever it was only meant to maim you, not kill you, if they were only using birdshot.''

"No." He sipped from a glass of wine she had given him. "I have no local lady friends, Deirdre. I haven't been a saint, but I've taken my fun far from here, and there's been nothing serious. Until now." She turned and saw that he looked at her with love.

Dinner was a bit awkward, but she made it less so by sitting cross-legged on the floor beside him as if they were at a picnic.

"I had things all set up for a romantic evening," he said, his expression moody. "Candles, music . . ."

"I know. I saw them when I went for your clothes. Sam, I'm sorry, too, that it didn't work out. But we have a lot of time.''

He looked at her and hoped in his heart that she was speaking the truth.

Deirdre cleaned up from dinner, wondering at the vulnerability she had seen in his eyes. Knowing that she did love him put matters in an entirely new perspective. She could no longer think selfishly, worrying about her own future alone. If what she felt for him was real, she wanted to behave in ways that would benefit him. His ego as well as his legs had taken punishment tonight, and if she could figure out how to do it, she would do what she could tonight to restore some of his sense of self-respect.

Just before she finished the dishes, the phone rang. It was Andy, wanting to report to Sam. In spite of her protests, he walked stiffly into the living room and took the call. She heard murmured words, an occasional curse, and then the sound of the receiver being replaced. Sam didn't return to the kitchen.

She put away her apron, turned out the lights, checked the door, which she locked carefully, and went into the bedroom. He was sprawled on top of the bedclothes, his head turned away from her. "Any news?" she asked.

Sam turned his head and looked at her. The only light left on in the house was the one by the bed. In spite of his pain and depression, he began to feel a rise of anticipation and excitement. Maybe she wasn't planning on mother-henning him, after all. "The highway patrol found the truck," he told her. "Stolen a few weeks ago from a rancher in Park County. The man had never even heard of me, much less had any reason to be involved in what happened."

"Fingerprints?" She walked over to the bed and sat on it. Sam reached for her hand.

"All over the place," he said, pulling her gently toward him. "Just like I'd like mine to be on you, lovely lady."

Deirdre touched his face. "Are you sure you'll be all right?"

"Honey, I was hit in the back, not the front." To demonstrate, he eased himself up and over her and kissed her. She responded with a willing eagerness. It wouldn't be as perfect and romantic as he had planned, Sam thought. But it would be *real*, and maybe in the long run that was more important than a carefully staged seduction.

Deirdre sighed as his weight settled on her, pressing her breasts against his chest. More than desire rose within her. She wanted to *give*. To love him until the world seemed right for him again. To give him pleasure and peace . . . anything he needed and wanted.

His kiss deepened, and she opened to him, wrapping her arms around his neck and weaving her fingers in his hair. His hand caressed her cheek, then moved down her throat and shoulder to cup her breast. She heard herself make a low sound and lifted herself to be touched.

Still stroking her gently, Sam rolled onto his side. "I want to see you," he murmured. "I know *I'm* not the prettiest sight in the world, but I want to leave the lights on while I undress you. All right?"

"It's all right." She kissed him. "And you'd be beautiful to me no matter what had happened." She touched his chest. "It's the man in here I care about."

Her words brought a tenderness to his desire. He slowly removed her sweater, whistling low at the lacy delight of a lilac bra that barely concealed her rounded breasts. He kissed each one in turn, making the peaks harden and feeling the flesh swell against his hand.

Deirdre expressed her pleasure, stroking his back and shoulders, then reaching up to remove the pajama top. Sam's chest was the picture of masculine beauty she had known it would be—muscled and covered with a light sprinkling of dark, curly hair that arrowed downward to a flat stomach. A puckered scar marred one shoulder just below the collarbone. His souvenir from Los Angeles, she decided. She touched it gently and then moved her fingers down to tease him from the top of his torso to the edge of the mysteries still covered by his pants.

"Mmmm." He closed his eyes for a moment,

savoring her caress. But eagerness to see her beauty uncovered drove him to take the lead again and to unfasten the silken bra.

Her breasts were feminine perfection to his eyes. Rounded and ivory-pale with light pink nipples, they beckoned him to taste and tease until she was crying out with pleasure. Sam moved his lips downward, seeking new delights.

Her body was slender without being too thin. Soft without being weak. He eased the jeans off, laughing when he saw that her panties matched the discarded bra. "You may have looked like the average Lodge Pole housewife out on an evening errand tonight," he said. "But underneath the camouflage, sex goddess!"

"We did have a date tonight," she reminded him. Further explanation of her attire fled as Sam began to worship the center of her, first through the silk, then without it. Deirdre grasped at his shoulders and threw her head back, giving in to the waves of pleasure his skillful touch brought her.

Sam deliberately took her to the brink, marveling at the responsiveness of her body to his touch. The blond-fringed triangle moistened and throbbed; he knew she was ready.

Deirdre helped him remove his pants, her entire body trembling with eagerness for union with his but her mind still concerned about his injuries. When she saw him naked, however, she knew she needn't have worried. His erect masculinity drew her hand to it like a magnet, and she began to pleasure him as he had done her.

Sam struggled for self-control. The sweetness of

her hands and lips were almost too much for him, and soon he cried out for her to take him inside of her before it was too late. Laughing, she opened to him and encircled him with her arms.

But when he entered her silkiness, he felt he had crossed into another dimension. Strength rushed into his body, and he had the control to fill her slowly, letting her tissues adjust and stretch to accommodate him. And then, the heaven of feeling himself touch the ultimate center of her.

Deirdre felt the thrum and pulse of pleasure begin. A small, rational part of her mind kept her from winding her legs around his injured thighs, but she couldn't control the lift and roll of her hips. Sam's body and the whispered words of endearment he breathed into her ear were bringing her to a level of passion that was almost frantic.

Then he seemed to fire with the same flame. His arms lifted her against him, and his loving became wild and strong. She heard herself scream as an impossible convulsion of delight took her again and again. Sam called her name, and she felt his body tighten, stiffen, and swell to bursting within her. His surge brought her back to the heights, and together they soared into the oneness of shared love.

THIRTEEN

Deirdre had never been loved the way Sam loved her. He seemed inexhaustible, the scope of his lovemaking limited only by his injury. It was nearly dawn before they finally fell asleep, wrapped in each other's arms.

The ringing of the telephone in the living room woke Deirdre, and she opened her eyes to see the bedroom washed in afternoon sunlight. Sam slumbered on.

She grabbed her robe and hurried into the living room, shutting the door so her conversation wouldn't disturb him. After everything—*everything!*—that had happened last night, she knew he needed all the rest he could get. She herself still felt weary and tender in a certain place. She picked up the receiver.

"I'm not mad." It was her father. "But I just can't figure how you were foolish enough to be photographed in a compromising—"

"He didn't!" Deirdre put her hand to her tangled hair.

"Whatever you mean, Deirdre," Richard Wilcox went on, "there's a picture of you kissing some big guy dressed in a policeman's uniform in this copy of a Los Angeles newspaper I'm holding in my hand." He cleared his throat. "I can't begin to tell you about the razzing I've—"

"Dad, I'm sorry. I had no idea any editor would print the thing, and there was no way we could stop the photographer once he'd taken the shot. Oh, Sam's going to be just furious."

"Sam, I assume," her father said dryly, "is the larger half of this epic clinch."

"You are mad." She sat down on the sofa. What an aggravating turn of events. And it would be even more so if her father found out that the "larger half" had made love to her for most of last night and even now lay sprawled in sleep on her bed. "Dad, it was an unavoidable, malicious accident, and if there were any way to undo it, believe me—"

"Malicious?"

Deirdre sighed. Then she explained in detail about Henderson and the strange little reporter. She did not tell him about the attack on Sam.

"I sent you there to *rest*," Richard shouted. "I was told that this . . . this Cassidy had the town so settled down that it was an event for a chicken to cross the road!"

"He does!" Deirdre answered shout for shout. "He's the finest policeman I've ever met. He uses his head, not his fists or his gun."

"Deirdre, I haven't read this article closely, just

skimmed it, but from what I got out of it, the man behaved suicidally in an incident in Los Angeles several years ago.''

"He saved lives, Dad.''

There was a pause on the line. Then she heard him sigh. ''Baby . . .'' he said, using a term of endearment she hadn't heard from him in years, ''when are you coming home?''

"Daddy, I don't know.''

"Is it this man?''

"I think I love him, Dad.''

It took a while to talk her father out of a state of apoplexy, but Deirdre finally managed to convince him that she hadn't lost her sense of perspective, and that Sam was not the heroic cretin that the news article by Tad Browning had painted him as. The reporter, she decided, was the one with the loose screw, judging from the way he had treated Sam. She assured her father that she would do nothing impulsively. At that point, she glanced guiltily at the bedroom door.

"I've even been to an internist over in Jackson,'' she added. ''He checked me over and gave me a good report. There's going to be stress no matter where I eventually decide to live, but I've learned some important lessons about relaxing out here.''

"From this Cassidy fellow?'' Richard Wilcox sounded angry again.

"It's the life here,'' she explained, holding on to her patience. ''You can go horseback riding and see land completely untouched by man. I've learned to fly-fish. This fall, I'll probably learn to hunt game. Dad, it's really a wonderful place to live. And the people are so friendly. I don't feel at all like an outsider.''

"I just want you to be happy and healthy.''

"I know.''

She wound up the conversation and hung up just as there was a knock at her front door. Hurrying to it, she found Andy standing outside.

"Come on in,'' she said. "Sam's still asleep, but I can give him a message if you'd like.''

Andy only glanced at her attire. The fact that his chief was asleep in her bedroom and she wore only a bathrobe didn't seem to faze him. "We still don't have any solid leads,'' he said. "Henderson seems to have an alibi. Some little gal says she was with him at the time it happened, and that Browning creep was flying back to L.A. I crawled all over old man Salters, and I don't think he had anything to do with it. Matter of fact, he's so upset he wants to talk to Sam personal.''

"Really?''

"He's waiting down at the station in case Sam felt like meeting with him.''

An idea began to form in Deirdre's mind. "Do you think he'd talk to me?'' she asked.

Andy shrugged. "I suppose so. But why would you . . .?''

"Trust me.'' She guided him into the kitchen and made them both a cup of coffee. Then she told him to wait for a few minutes while she dressed.

Moving quietly so as not to wake Sam, she took a quick shower to remove the muskiness that clung to her from the night's activities. She put on a minimum of makeup and dressed in a conservative gray, pin-striped suit, topping the outfit off with a pale-pink blouse. Businesslike but feminine. She checked herself approvingly in the mirror. Do the hair in a twist, she decided.

Before she left, she went over to Sam and kissed his cheek softly. He was still deeply asleep. She adjusted the sheet and gave the back of his legs a quick inspection. The bandages looked clean and were all still in place. Amazing, she thought, remembering his exertions. Sam Cassidy was something else again!

Andy drove her to the station, and she explained to him that she intended to do what she could to shake Salters to make him put pressure on Bud Henderson. She was certain in her mind that the foreman had been the one to shoot Sam.

Andy opened the door for her, and she strode in as if she owned the place, taking a seat at Sam's desk before acknowledging the presence of the gray-haired man who had risen from the extra chair when she had entered. She folded her hands on the table and regarded him. Andy lounged against the wall near the door.

Salters was a man of indeterminate age. Life as a rancher had weathered his skin, but his body seemed trim and fit. He held his hat in his hands, and her scrutiny was clearly making him uncomfortable. His booted feet made creaking sounds as he shifted his weight from one to the other.

Finally Deirdre spoke, using the cold, personal-attack style she had seen in hundreds of Senate hearings. "Mr. Salters, now that I've seen you in person, I really fail to understand how a man who seems as fit and competent as yourself finds it necessary to employ a troublemaker like Bud Henderson."

"Ma'am, he's a good foreman." Salters began to look defiant.

"Are you aware that this 'good foreman' was partly responsible for a most embarrassing situation to arise that caused my father to call me all the way from Washington, D.C., this morning?"

"Your father?"

"Senator Wilcox." Deirdre kept her expression cool, but let her eyes accuse the man in front of her.

"Miss Wilcox, I . . ."

"Sit down, Mr. Salters," she ordered. He obeyed. She filled him in on what had happened with Henderson and the reporter, noting that Salter's expression changed to one of outrage as the facts unfolded.

"I got a daughter," he said when she had finished. "Married and lives down in Cheyenne, and if anybody did that to her, I'd tear the skunk in two!"

"I think you understand how my father feels, then," she replied. "Sam is still unaware that the story and picture have been published, but I imagine you know how he will react."

"How bad was he hurt?" Concern showed on his face. Maybe, Deirdre decided, he didn't like Sam but did respect him.

"Badly enough to still be bedridden." It was a partial lie, she knew. Sam would have been here if it hadn't been for the love he lavished on her for so many hours. Memory made her tingle.

Salters turned from her to look at Andy. "How airtight is Henderson's alibi?" he asked.

"As airtight as Molly Jones. That's who he claimed he was with, and she backs him."

"Would she hold up under interrogation?" Deirdre asked. "*Real* interrogation?"

The three of them discussed the case for a while longer, but Deirdre knew that she had accomplished what she had come to do—make Salters put pressure on Henderson. The rancher was too wise to shelter a man who might have committed an armed attack on a law officer, even if he had gone to the trouble of getting the foreman off on the simple assault charges. Bud Henderson's days at the ranch were numbered, and she hoped that would mean the man would move on and not cause Sam any further grief.

Sam woke, feeling disoriented for a moment. He had been having a nightmare, and it extended into reality. The back of his legs were on fire! Then he remembered.

Remembered it all. Remembered Deirdre's sweetness and sensuality. The loving they had shared. He raised himself up on slightly chapped elbows and looked around.

She wasn't in the bedroom, and he couldn't hear her anywhere in the house. Glancing at the clock on her bedside table, he saw that it was after four. God, he'd slept the day through.

With an effort, he got out of the bed and made his way to the bathroom where he bathed out of the sink, taking care to keep the bandages on his legs dry. It could have been worse, he thought. He could have left his posterior out to be pelted with the birdshot. That would have been doubly humiliating.

He found his bathrobe and put it on, then checked throughout the house. She was definitely gone, and he felt a pang that she had neglected to leave him a note. She had made incredible love to him, but he wondered if she felt anything more than affection for him. Women could enjoy sex without emotional commitment, he knew. But he hoped in his heart that Deirdre was different. At least with him.

A rumble from his stomach told him that he needed food, so he returned to the kitchen and built a sandwich from the meager offerings in her refrigerator. When she did return—he assumed she was at the office—he hoped she would remember to bring more food. Better yet, he should have her go over and empty out his larder. Now that he had managed to get into her home, he didn't plan to move out until he knew which way their relationship was going.

Home, he thought, munching on the sandwich. Home. Family. Was he, the confirmed bachelor, actually beginning to think along those lines? Could he possibly imagine Deirdre willing to marry him, settle down here, and have children? The idea literally made the hair on the back of his neck stand up. *Slow down,* he cautioned himself. *You've been her lover for one night. Wait and see what happens.*

The phone rang, and he went into the living room to answer it, thinking it had to be Deirdre. He said hello eagerly.

"Cassidy?" The voice was muffled, and Sam felt his insides chill.

"This is Chief Cassidy," he replied. "Who's this?"

"You were lucky," the voice went on. "That was

just a warning, though. Next time the gun might be loaded with buckshot.'' A pause. ''And I might aim at the little blond honey instead of you.'' The receiver clicked before Sam could reply.

With shaking fingers, Sam dialed the office. Andy answered.

''Where's Deirdre?'' Sam shouted.

''She said she needed to shop, so I loaned her my—''

''Listen to me, and don't interrupt.'' Sam told him of the threatening call. ''I want one of us sticking to her like glue until we catch who's at the bottom of this.'' Andy assured him that he was on his way.

Sam put the receiver down and ran a hand through his hair. Damn, he thought. Now whoever was after him was using her to harass him. It *had* to be Henderson. No one else held a grudge that included both of them. He wondered if he should send her away to keep her safe, even though the idea hurt him. Once away, he couldn't be sure she would ever come back.

He started to sit on the sofa, then thought better of it. Worry for Deirdre's safety had temporarily taken his mind off his own troubles. The wounds itched, but he kept himself from touching them. The faster he healed, the better he would be able to protect her.

The phone rang again, and he grabbed it, swearing at the caller and calling him a lousy coward for not daring to face him openly. When he paused for breath, searching his mind for further insults, he heard a rich, deep voice with a southern accent ask him if he was finished.

Sam swallowed hard. "Who is this?" he asked, already knowing the answer.

"I'm Richard Wilcox," the new caller said. "Deirdre's father. And I sincerely hope that a man with a vocabulary like yours isn't a close acquaintance of my daughter."

Oh, brother, Sam thought. He leaned gingerly against the sofa. "Senator Wilcox, I'm Sam Cassidy." He listened as the senator swore roundly.

"What're you doing in Deirdre's house?" Wilcox asked finally. "It's bad enough that you compromised her in the picture, but to—"

"Picture?" Sam felt ice rush through him once more. It couldn't be . . . .

But it was. The senator explained about the article, leaving no doubt in Sam's mind that Tad Browning had slipped a cog and done an about-face on him. The little man had worshipped him in print once. Now he was making a fool of him. Sam wasn't sure which he disliked most. And changes worried him.

"What I would like to suggest," Wilcox said, "is that we three send letters to the editor, complaining about this sensational type of journalism. If we can put enough pressure on him, maybe he'll make the reporter print an apology."

"Senator, knowing the man, I doubt he'll change his tune. You have no idea how much he embarrassed me . . . ."

"Oh, but I do. Earlier today when I heard my little girl tell me that she believed she loved you, I sent out for anything that I could find out about you. I read the account of the incident in Los Angeles.

Several accounts, in fact, and it's clear that particular reporter made you his personal idol. That he turned on you now isn't surprising." He continued on, explaining his theory of hero worship and its reversal.

Sam barely heard. Deirdre had told her father that she *loved* him. Well, *believed* she loved him, but that was good enough for Sam. He sat, ignoring the pain in his thighs. The joy in his heart was too great.

"Cassidy," the senator said, getting his attention again. "I know Deirdre's a grown woman, but I can't help worrying. What are your intentions toward my daughter? I find you're at her house. Makes a father wonder what's going on."

Sam hesitated, then plunged. Senator Wilcox did have a right to know at least about the shooting and the threats. He started with the night at the Alibi and took him all the way to the present, leaving out only the personal details.

"I need your advice, sir," he added. "Should I ship Deirdre home for her own safety? I love her, too, and I don't want anything at all to happen to her."

"A politician and his family live with the possibility of some crazy taking a pot shot at them all the time, son." Richard Wilcox sounded friendlier. "I don't think either of us could make her run scared. She'll stand her ground with you, unless I miss my guess by a country mile."

"She'll be constantly guarded," Sam assured him. "I have another officer with her right now."

"Give her a gun," the senator advised. "She knows how to use one." Sam agreed to that.

"As for my intentions," he said. "Senator, for

the first time in my life, I'm thinking about marriage and a family. I just don't know if she'd be happy out here away from all the action she's known.''

"Don't sell your neck of the woods short, son. You should have heard the snow job she gave me. Riding, fishing, hunting. Sounds like a great place to live.''

"It is.'' Sam felt his inner joy grow even greater.

Deirdre sat impatiently in the passenger seat as Andy loaded the groceries into the back of his pickup. He had appeared at her heels while she had been shopping and insisted that he had direct orders from Sam not to let her out of his sight, but he wouldn't give her any explanation. She wondered if last night's intimacies had addled Sam's brain and was determined to give him a piece of her mind when she got home to help clear his. They might be lovers, but he did not own her, for goodness' sake!

Andy seemed to sense her annoyance, because he kept reassuring her it was for a good reason that he stay with her until she was safely back with Sam.

"What do you mean 'safely?' '' she snapped. "I've been taking care of myself for a long time, Andy. Just because Sam and I . . .'' She broke off, blushing at what she had nearly blurted out.

But Andy didn't laugh or leer at her as she had expected. Instead he spoke seriously. "It's because Sam cares so much for you that this is necessary,'' he said.

Surprised, she turned and looked at him. "How do you know how he feels?''

Andy grinned. "I'm a trained observer, Miss Wilcox,'' he said in a theatrical tone. "I can read people like books.''

"Don't tease me, Andy.''

He slowed the pickup, and she realized they had been heading for Sam's place instead of her own. "I've got to bring a few things to Sam," he explained. "As for teasing you, I'm sorry. But it's true. I've known Sam for quite a while. When he looks at you, he sees stars. You're very special to him, Deirdre.''

He insisted that she accompany him inside, saying that Sam would skin him if he left her alone outside. Curiosity growing, Deirdre pumped questions at him to no avail. But when she saw what he had come by to collect, she began to get the picture.

Andy took Sam's holster and revolver from his bureau top, gathered up a box of shells, and then took a rifle from behind the bedroom door. When he searched Sam's closet until he found a bullet-proof vest, Deirdre was certain.

"We've both been threatened," she stated, confronting the blond man. "Someone—the person who shot Sam—has made another threat. And this time, I'm included, aren't I?''

The look on Andy's face answered her question.

FOURTEEN

He need not have worried about Deirdre, Sam decided. The warrior aspect of her personality that had surfaced during the Alibi fight had returned with a vengeance. She accepted the .38 revolver and made no objections to being measured for a protective vest. She also agreed wholeheartedly to the condition that she be under guard at all times, only she made it clear that he was also to submit to that condition.

"No wandering off, riding Licorice on your own," she declared, her hands on her hips. The holstered revolver riding the waistband of her jeans looked incongruous on her feminine figure, but the determined expression on her delicate features told him that she meant business. "No patroling alone," she added. "When you go out, I go shotgun, understand?"

"Yes, ma'am!" Sam made a little bow. "Your command is my wish."

"You are taking this seriously, aren't you?" Her eyes narrowed, and Sam found himself wondering just who was the real Guardian Angel.

Deirdre waited for his answer. He was just the type to go set himself up as a target to draw the enemy away from her, and she wasn't going to let him do that. Not when it might end in the destruction of the man she loved.

"I am," he said, coming over and taking her in his arms. "You see, I have so much to live for now." He put a finger under her chin and lifted it, placing a gentle kiss on her lips. "I love you, Deirdre," he said softly.

"Sam!" She flung her arms around him. "I love you, too!"

He laughed. "I know. Your father told me."

"My . . . father?"

Sam explained about the senator's call and his suggestion that they compose letters of objection to the article. She agreed with no hesitation and immediately sat down at the kitchen table to start composing. They worked together and had the document finished in less than thirty minutes. Then a knock at the door startled them both.

"You stay put," Sam ordered. "I'll get it."

"No deal." She stood and drew her gun. "Remember the rules."

As it turned out, their caller was totally innocent. Sally had sent Julie up with a pot of stew and a note saying that she hoped Sam was feeling better. Deirdre accepted the meal with gratitude, knowing that in her emotional state she would likely ruin anything she tried to cook tonight. Their mutual declaration of love on top of all the other things had made her feel that the world was coming crazily unglued, and she had welcomed the interlude of letter-composing, using the time to do a bit of mental composing and calming as well.

Sam watched as she moved around the kitchen, setting up for the meal. If the weapon were ignored, she could be one of the many housewives in Lodge Pole engaged in the same activity at about this time. The idea of marriage again rose in his mind, but he dismissed bringing it up. It was still far too early.

He sat gingerly on a pillow while they ate, and Deirdre went over what had happened in the office with Old Man Salters again. Andy had given him a full report when he had come by with Deirdre and the groceries, but Sam found hearing the story from her gave him a deeper perspective. He agreed that the best approach would be to see if Henderson's alibi could be broken. The girl would be brought in for thorough interrogation first thing in the morning, he declared. He also decided that he had better ask the sheriff for the temporary loan of another officer. To have this problem right in the middle of the tourist season was the worst possible timing.

"You know," Deirdre said, stirring the tasty stew with her fork. "Between my causing Henderson grief through Salters and your doing the same by working on his girlfriend, we might rattle his cage hard enough to make him run for it. Maybe we won't have to act like a besieged—"

"Don't start thinking that way." Sam spoke harshly. "He's a vindictive man, more likely to attack than flee."

"And Browning?" She waved at the letter lying on the counter. "Our letters aren't liable to win his friendship, either. If he was somehow responsible—"

"He could have hired it done," Sam agreed thoughtfully. "In fact, they could both have conspired to do it. The birdshot touch is a little too creative for Henderson's mind. I would have expected him to blast me to hell and gone first time. This wounding and telephone threat amounts to torture, both mental and physical. Henderson doesn't have the cunning for that unaided."

Deirdre's brow wrinkled slightly. "I hate to admit it, Sam. But for the first time, I'm starting to feel scared." He reached over and took her hand, squeezing it reassuringly.

"I'll take care of you," he said. Deirdre believed him.

Later that night she tended his injuries, removing the bandages and gently rubbing the ointment over the back of his thighs and calves. To her relief, it seemed that healing had already begun. Sam was a very healthy specimen, she reminded herself. She expected his body to take care of itself quickly.

After that, they indulged in a less lengthy replay of last night's passionate activity. When they crested together, she wept for the sheer joy of knowing he loved her.

Morning brought a return to routine. She helped him into his uniform, sympathizing when he gritted his teeth as he pulled on his pants.

But she felt no sympathy at all for the young woman Andy brought into the station about an hour later. Molly Jones was a slutty, sullen person, and

Deirdre sensed instantly that she was lying. How, she wondered, had Henderson managed to get her to alibi for him. Money? Threats? It surely couldn't have been for love. Although Molly was attractive in an overstuffed, frowzy way, she didn't strike Deirdre as the type of woman who would care about anyone but herself.

It turned out that she didn't. Sam and Andy lit into her, and Deirdre watched, fascinated as the team of men tore the girl's lie apart bit by bit. Finally, she admitted the truth: that Bud Henderson had come by her place outside of Jackson a good hour after Sam was shot. He had given her money to cover for him. They had been lovers in a sense, but she told the policemen that lately she had been trying to avoid him. He frightened her. Sam had promised to ask the Jackson police to provide her with protection until Henderson was apprehended. Then he issued the order for the man's arrest, calling the sheriff, since the Three Diamond Ranch was in county jurisdiction.

During the afternoon the news came from the sheriff's department that Henderson had been fired by Salters the day before and had disappeared. Deirdre felt a sense of relief, hoping that it did indeed mean that her wish that the man would just go away had turned true. Sam, however, wasn't as optimistic.

"He's holed up," he declared. "Waiting for another chance at us, and this time of the year, he could be anywhere." She saw a calculating gleam in his green eyes.

Apparently so had Andy. "Forget what you're thinking, Chief," he said, his tone determined enough to make both Sam and Deirdre stare at him. "I won't let you go riding off into the mountains alone, and I won't leave Deirdre to go with you. We don't have enough of a case to call for an all-out man hunt. Molly could change her tune anytime, and you know that.''

Sam deflated and sat down. "You're right," he admitted. "All we can do is stay alert and wait."

And that was what they did for a full month. July became August, and tourists passed through Lodge Pole in droves, keeping Sam, Deirdre, and Andy busy with minor police business. The case of Bud Henderson never left her mind, but Deirdre found that she was able to live with the need to be wary but not worried. She had her own abilities, and Sam was always there to protect her.

Their love had grown stronger as the days passed. Yielding to logic, she moved in with him after his legs healed. Sam's home was his own territory, and it only made sense that they would be safer there. Besides, Sam declared, Licorice was the best damn watch horse in the world. No stranger would get within fifty yards of the place without her sounding off.

Before she finally closed up the Thorton place, Deirdre called her father and gave him her new phone number and address.

"So you really are throwing in your lot with the lawman," Richard asked, no reproach in his voice. "I suppose that means I've got to come out and meet the man."

"We *aren't* marrying. The move made sense for a number of reasons, safety primary among them."

Sam leaned against the rail on the front porch. He

had gone outside to give her as much privacy as possible, but he could still overhear the conversation. When she had made the comment about not marrying, he felt an ache begin inside him. Was it just the challenge of finally falling in love with a woman who wanted to keep her independence, he wondered. Was that what was making him so hot on the idea of a permanent relationship, legalized? Or was he really ready. Ready in a psychological and biological sense to become a family man. Sam smiled at the thought.

"That's a pleasant expression." Deirdre's voice and touch on his arm startled him out of his reverie. "Could I offer a penny for the thought behind it?"

Sam shook his head. "My secret," he said, putting his arm around her shoulders. He'd win her, no matter what it took. He promised himself that as he looked down into the shining skies of her eyes.

As they rode back to the station, Deirdre told him that her father had learned that Tad Browning had been dropped from the paper's staff after he had refused to print an apology. She credited her father's influence with the action, but said that perhaps the editor was a góod newsman, and that when he realized that Browning was using the paper to get at Sam for personal, if weird, reasons, he canned him in order to avoid similar situations in the future.

"So now Browning has a concrete reason to hate me," Sam said quietly. "An unsound mind with a solid motive is a dangerous combination. Let's hope that he and Henderson have no way to get back together, honey." He reached for her hand, and the warmth of his touch eased the chill that had gone through her at his words.

Chills, however, were the least of their problems for the days ahead. Unseasonably dry weather and hot daytime temperatures caused Lodge Pole to simmer under an unaccustomed heat wave, and the mountain community, unused to such weather, had difficulty adjusting. In cooperation with the county and the fire department, which consisted of one rather elderly truck and two volunteers, Sam enforced rigid fire control and water restrictions which grated on everyone's nerves, especially campers who used the designated grounds within the town's limits to set up for the night. Campfires were out, Sam declared. He would only allow cooking in metal grills and made certain that they were monitored carefully. Following him on his rounds, as had become their custom, Deirdre often had to hide an amused smile as she listened to The Guardian dictate to an irate out-of-stater the rules and regulations and the reasons for them.

"This is National Forest land," Sam would say patiently. "By imposing fire restrictions until we get a break in the weather, we are all doing ourselves a favor. Try to think patriotically." As they moved on, Deirdre would frequently hear mutterings about police-state tactics. But no one ever called Sam's hand.

And it was no wonder, she mused. The bullet-proof vest made him look even bigger, and he had taken to carrying a riot gun as well as his regular hand revolver. He was imposing.

She, on the other hand, had taken one glance in the mirror at herself in the make-do uniform and vest that Sam had ordered her to wear whenever they were out and had collapsed in helpless laughter. If only her society friends could see her now, they would not recognize her, and if they did . . .!

The vest made her look downright busty and put about ten pounds on her trim figure. The straw cowboy hat wasn't so bad, but because of the heat, she had braided her hair to keep the heavy mane off of her neck and shoulders. Since she had to wear the hat, the only way she could wear the braids was hanging straight down. It made her look like a little girl trying to pass for an adult. But when Sally had seen her, she had nodded approval and given her a pair of beaded braid tassels that she said had been made by a Shohone woman she knew. Deirdre accepted the gift with gratitude, sensing that Sally was parting with something precious to her. She wore them proudly but knew her sophisticated friends back East would find them droll.

Her legs and hips looked fine in the jeans and boots that were standard for the Lodge Pole force, but she couldn't get used to the uniform shirt or the small badge she had to wear in order to make her hand gun legal in the town limits. Sam had had her sworn in as an assistant officer-in-training by the council, so Deirdre Wilcox, late of the office of Senator Wilcox of Georgia, graduate in art history from Georgetown University, assistant curator at a prestigious Washington art gallery, was now officially a cop. In Lodge Pole, Wyoming.

Her skin was tanned from the hours in the sun, and she rarely wore makeup now. It didn't seem to fit her new role. And then Sam *had* said that the blue shirt made her eyes brighter than sapphires. If he liked the way she looked, she was satisfied. Only Sam's opinion mattered to her anymore because of her deep love for him.

They had little time for relaxing, but they had a mutual agreement that no matter how busy they were, or how tired, there would be that special time of sharing before they slept. Sharing physically, emotionally, and forging themselves closer and closer with each bonding.

As the days passed, Deirdre began to realize that she could probably never leave Sam and that she ought to start thinking about a permanent relationship with him. Not being sure how he really felt about marriage, however, and restrained by the old social mores she had been taught as a young girl, she knew that she would have to wait until he brought it up. If, indeed, he ever would. Until then, she was content to be his lover and constant companion.

One particularly hot evening, after they had made rounds and had turned the night over to Andy, she stood in the stifling bedroom and stripped off her clothes and armament. Sam stood in the doorway, grinning as he watched the sight.

"You make one gorgeous little lady cop," he drawled. "But I prefer you *au naturel* myself."

Deirdre smiled back. "I'm going to shower August off me. Care to join in?"

Sam hesitated. Showering together left them both vulnerable, and although he longed for the sensual ecstasy that would come from the experience, he declined. "I'll go drink a beer and sit out on the front porch and wait my turn." He lifted his riot gun, and she nodded understanding.

As she showered, she felt a bitterness at the two men who literally were keeping them hostages in their own home. She knew that the strain was telling on Sam. It showed in his face. She had been too caught up in the new life and love to be very depressed about it, but now and then she felt this anger. Should she ever have Bud Henderson under her gun again, she wasn't sure that she could trust herself to react with control.

She unbound her braids and washed her hair, knowing how Sam loved to tangle his hands in it when they loved. Since his legs had healed completely, there seemed no end to his passionate imagination, and she felt herself start to tingle in anticipation as she stepped from the shower.

She wrapped her hair in a towel, pulled on a light bathrobe, and went into the bedroom to comb the tangled strands out. A light breeze had begun to blow in the two opened windows, and she felt a sense of relief that the night might cool down. She took the towel off and fluffed her wet hair, momentarily blinded by the strands.

Suddenly she was caught in a powerful, hurtful embrace, and a wet rag was forced over her face. The smell from the rag made her choke, and she struggled for air. Then all was darkness.

Sam sipped his beer slowly, letting his tired body relax in the pleasant evening air. Tonight, he decided, he would put out some feelers to Deirdre about the possibility of making what they had between them a permanent commitment. This business with Henderson was eating away at him, and he knew that he needed the honesty with her that she had asked for in the beginning. He needed to let her know exactly what he was thinking and feeling, regardless of what her reaction might be.

Sam sighed and took another sip. He couldn't go the old-fashioned way and get her pregnant, he thought wryly. He knew she popped one of those damn little pills every day. Smart lady. Sometimes too darn smart. If they did marry, he'd have his work cut out for him for a lifetime. And he knew he'd love every minute of it.

From the direction of the corral, he heard Licorice make a whickering sound. Still carrying the gun, he got up and ambled over to where the horse stood near the fence.

"Guess I'll have to buy you a roommate, old girl," he said, rubbing the mare's nose affectionately. "If we have ourselves a permanent human resident, she'll need a mount to ride for our evening outings." The mare blew through her soft lips.

Sam laughed. "I guess that means 'what outings?' and I deserve it." Since the telephone call, he hadn't taken his nightly rounds on Licorice, leaving the exercising of the animal up to Tommy Edwards during the day. *Damn*, he thought. *I almost wish something would happen to finish the whole business off right now.*

Licorice whickered again, this time the sound closer to a full neigh. Sam frowned. The mare was shifting from one foot to the other and nudging at him with her nose over the fence.

"Deirdre?" he called.

No answer.

Sam dropped the beer can and ran back to the

house, thumbing the safety off the riot gun as he went. He burst through the open front door and raced into the bedroom, weapon at ready.

The room was empty, and the reek of chloroform hit him like a slap in the face. Her revolver was on the bedside table, but both windows were open, and Sam could see that the screen on the one facing the woods was missing. Not something a woman just coming from a refreshing shower would notice.

Hope dying, he looked in the bathroom. Empty, as he had known it would be. Anguish filled him, and then he moved over to the window.

The night was dark, and the wind picking up, but he believed with a flashlight and one of Doc Turner's tracking dogs, he might be able to catch them before anything serious happened to her. He reached for the phone, but as his fingers touched the receiver, it began to ring. Slowly, Sam picked it up.

"Cassidy?" Muffled voice again. "We have your lady. If you don't want her harmed, don't try to follow. Get in touch with her senator father, tell him what's happened, and tell the old man that we'll be in touch with ransom demands."

"Listen, you—!"

"No tricks, Cassidy. No heroics, or Miss Wilcox will be found floating down the Snake River. Understand?"

Mutely, Sam nodded.

FIFTEEN

"Chief Cassidy? Sam?"

Sam turned and recognized Deirdre's father immediately. The senator was striding across the floor of the small airport just outside of Jackson with the same imperious look that his daughter often had. Although male and grayhaired, there was no mistaking the family resemblance. Blood will tell, Sam thought.

He held out his hand, and Richard Wilcox took it, giving a warm, firm clasp. Sam glanced inquiringly at the two men flanking the senator. "F.B.I?" he asked, knowing the answer before he asked the question.

Both men nodded, producing badges. Sam considered drawing his revolver and ordering the pair of three-piece suiters back on the private plane that had brought Wilcox, but he knew that impulsive behavior would get him nowhere. "Gentlemen . . ." he acknowledged tightly.

He led the trio wordlessly out of the airport and over to his Jeep. The front of the vehicle was still pockmarked by the birdshot that had hit him in the legs. *As soon as this crisis is over*, he promised the Jeep silently, *you'll get the best damn body job available*.

When everyone was seated—the senator beside Sam and the two federal men in back—Sam turned and faced them all.

"I didn't want to start any conversation while we were in public," he said, looking from one man to the other. "And I know kidnapping makes this a federal jurisdiction case, but, Senator Wilcox, these two men are city cops, and they aren't going to be able to find their own—"

"I know." Wilcox held up a conciliatory hand. The two men in the back were silent. "Sam, they're window dressing, and they have agreed to let you handle things. Once Deirdre is free and the kidnappers caught—"

"Then you men had better take over!" Sam started his engine. "Because I'm liable to tear them apart with my bare hands."

He calmed down as they drove and began to explain his theories to the three easterners. Every bit of his deduction, he admitted, was based completely on conjecture. The only hard evidence he and Andy had found were some hairs and bits of dirt on the floor where Deirdre had struggled momentarily with her captors before succumbing to the drug. "But unless we catch them with her, we won't have a case that will stand up in court," he said bitterly. "A good lawyer will make it seem that Deirdre could have invited someone in while I was out."

"But if the hairs do match one of the kidnappers, and you do catch them with her," one of the F.B.I. men interjected, "then I'll guarantee you a solid case."

Sam glanced back at him. "You're a lawyer?"

The man blushed slightly. "I did get a degree before joining the department."

Sam gave him a second glance. The man was young, true, but he was well built and had an intelligent look in his eyes. "Well," Sam muttered, "you'd better keep close tabs on me, lawyer, because I don't want to blow this case on a technicality."

The agent promised.

Deirdre fought the nausea that her headache was causing her and struggled against the ropes that bound her wrists and ankles. She had awakened a few hours before to find herself the captive of Bud Henderson and his huge friend, Luke. She was wrapped lightly in a blanket and lying on her side, facing a campfire. The two men were across the fire from her, eating and talking.

"You really think this reporter guy can be trusted?" Luke was asking Bud. The big man munched on what looked like a piece of jerky, and Deirdre's stomach contracted, reminding her how long it had been since she had eaten.

"Without him, we wouldn't have had a snowball's chance in hell of pulling this off," Henderson replied. "We coulda just shot the broad," he said in an offhand way that made Deirdre grow cold in spite of the warmth from the blanket and fire. "But *this* way, we get cold hard cash out of the deal."

She lay still. No mention of whether she was going to be released alive. Deirdre remembered Sam saying that his old department's policy was to consider a hostage as already dead. Maybe the same theory should be applied to her situation. Kidnapping, she knew, was a federal offense, and she could identify the criminals. Even Browning, from the conversation she had overheard.

Thinking of Sam she knew he was moving heaven and earth to find her, but it was almost an impossible situation. She had no idea where they were, but she knew she had been taken many miles back into the wilderness, and if a full-scale hunt was made for her, her captors were sure to kill her and run. Sam would know that. She worked again at the ropes.

Just outside of Lodge Pole, the radio in the Jeep signaled Sam to answer. he picked up the microphone and spoke his call number.

"Chief . . ." Andy's voice came clearly over the speaker. "This may mean nothing, but one of the rangers up on Red Tops reported seeing a campfire plume just south of his tower. Says he can't make out any people because of the trees, but it's the only smoke he's seen since the ban on fires this month."

Sam felt an exaltation rise in him. "Get in touch with two other towers," he commanded. "See if you can get a triangulation."

"Check, Chief. Out."

Sam hung up the microphone and looked at Richard Wilcox. "The two lugs that snatched her aren't all that bright, Senator," he said, grinning for the first time since his love had been taken.

"But the third one?" Richard Wilcox's face looked worried

Sam drove into town. "If we get a triangulation, I'm going in alone on horseback," he said. "I'll have to trust your years of experience in dealing with people to help you handle Browning when he contacts you. He mustn't suspect that we have any leads or he may pull the plug on the whole operation." He pulled up to the station, and the four of them sat for a moment in silence, contemplating what would happen in that case.

Deirdre sat where Henderson had propped her against a tree. Considering the man's probable intentions, he had treated her with astonishing politeness, untying her hands so that she could eat and drink— although he did secure her to the tree with a stout rope. Neither man really looked directly at her or spoke to her, making her feel more certain that they intended to kill her. Why be friendly, when you were going to shoot a person.

She shut her eyes and thought of Sam. If, somehow, she got out of this in one piece, she would immediately propose marriage to him, she swore to herself. Forget the rules. Forget the etiquette! She loved him, and she wanted to be by his side forever! Tears fell down her cheeks, but something inside her hardened. Sam would be trying to save her, but she should do something to help herself as well.

She opened her eyes and saw to her surprise that the two kidnappers were out of sight. Maybe answering calls of nature, she thought. And perhaps she had seemed safely asleep. She was tied tightly enough.

But her hands were free. She looked around the pine-needle-strewn ground, searching for some kind of a weapon. There was nothing but a few sticks and a cone or two. Nothing that could stand against a revolver and rifle. Then her eye was drawn to the fire.

Sam took one more look at the topography sheet that Andy had marked with the triangulation approximation. They had taken her into rough country, but they hadn't taken her far. Probably because they didn't want to be far from a good escape route. He rolled up the sheet, his thoughts grim. The freshening breeze brushed his cheek, and he longed for it to be Deirdre's touch that teased him. Looking at the sky for the first time, he sent up a prayer for her safety and then noticed that the blazing sun that had punished the area for so many weeks was hidden behind fat pewter-colored clouds. Oh no, he thought. If it started to rain, it would impede Licorice's progress and wash away trail signs. He kicked the mare, and they moved ahead at a faster pace.

Deirdre took careful aim and tossed another stick. The fire was spreading out of the contained area and licking hungrily at the dry pine needles on the forest floor. The wind was blowing away from her, and she prayed that it would continue to do so. Joan of Arc she did not need to be.

Soon the area was full of smoke. She coughed and choked, managing to stand and make her way around the tree until her back was to the clearing. She paid for the action with numerous cuts and bruises from the rope and the rough bark, but at least she now faced away from the flames. After a few minutes, she heard curses and cries, but neither man came to her to either shoot her or release her. The wind blew harder, and she began to freeze on one side while feeling the heat of the fire on the other. Deirdre prayed harder than she ever had in her life.

Suddenly the ropes binding her to the tree fell away, and she stumbled forward to land facedown on the ground. The fire, she realized muzzily, had severed her bonds. And if she didn't get her ankles free, it would take her life!

She struggled, ripping the skin of her hands on the rope, but managed to free herself in time to beat out a smoldering fringe on her bathrobe and take to her heels, running blindly in the direction of the cold wind, leaving the blanket behind to burn with her bonds.

She ran, stumbling on roots and rocks and cutting her bare feet on the rough ground but determined to keep up the punishing pace until she found safety. The pine trees flashed by, occasionally one ripping at her with a branch, tearing at her hair and robe. But she ran on.

Once she thought she heard a rumbling noise over the sound of her labored breathing. Her mind didn't register the meaning of the sound until cold rain began pelting down through the trees. Rain! Deirdre slowed and looked up.

Above her the sky was dark gray. One of the late summer cloudbursts that Sam had casually mentioned to her, she thought. A cloudburst that might stop the fire, but also might make it impossible for her to find her way out of the forest before cold and exposure did to her what her kidnappers and the fire had not. Survival and life itself now took on a fresh meaning. She pushed her streaming hair back from her face and forged ahead.

Sam kept up the fast pace he had held the mare to while he took out his rain slicker from his saddle bag. He tugged the garment into place and urged Licorice on. He had seen the billow of smoke before the rain had started, and it had seemed to be a beacon—one of hope mixed with alarm. A forest fire could force the kidnappers to flee their hideout, but would they take Deirdre with them? Now with the rain, he felt his hopes sinking even further. All of the horrors that could have happened to her kept running like a motion picture in his mind. Sam began to curse slowly and steadily, mixing the swear words with prayers. She was all he wanted in a wife, he thought miserably. If she were gone, he wasn't sure that life would be worth living.

Deirdre felt herself weakening. The strain of the last day, the effects of the drug, and the cold rain on her bruised and bleeding body were taking their toll. Once she stumbled, and it seemed to take her hours to force herself to a trembling standing position. She began to hold on to the trees to stay upright.

Sam. She thought his name over and over in her mind, and soon her lips were whispering it out loud. Sam. If she had one last sight to see before she died, she prayed it would be his face. The face of the man she loved.

Suddenly the trees failed her, and she fell to the ground, sprawling on wet grass. She rested her cheek against the cold wetness, smelling the earthy odors of plant and soil. Behind her shoulder, she could see the trees. She must be in one of the mountain meadows that had pleasured her so when she and Sam had taken rides. So long ago. She began to whisper his name again. The rain beat down on her.

Licorice nickered. Sam let her slow, trusting the animal's instincts far more than his own. If she heard something, it might be worth investigating. He gave the mare her head.

She made her way through the dripping trees, and Sam noted that the rain seemed to be getting harder. Probably hail next, he thought grimly. Licorice whinnied.

"It's going to be okay, girl," Sam murmured, patting the mare's wet neck. "We'll find her," he added, wishing he felt as confident as his words sounded. Licorice increased her pace, her ears twitching.

Deirdre opened her eyes. Something had stirred her to consciousness. Painfully, she lifted her head and looked up.

She was still in the meadow, and the rain that pelted down was mixed with hard little balls of hail.

Instinct told her to get back into the relative shelter of the trees. She forced herself to her knees.

But her muscles would take her no farther. *I'll just kneel in this place until I fall down dead,* she thought. Then she put all of her pain and anguish into one last cry.

"Sam!"

He heard that! Sam dug his heels into Licorice's side, and they raced in the direction of Deirdre's cry. Bursting through the trees, he spotted her, a slash of gold and white in the whiteness of the hailstorm, but outlined against the darkness of the forest. He called her name as Licorice raced across the open field toward her.

Deirdre heard his voice and knew that she was experiencing the last moments of her life. Thankful to have heard him in her mind, if not actually to have seen him, she let her body slump, resting one hand on the ground.

But the ground was . . . shaking. As if something huge ran toward her. Screening her eyes with her other hand, she lifted her head and saw an enormous black shape bearing down on her. Madness, she thought. And fainted.

Sam pulled Licorice to a skidding halt beside Deirdre's still form. He swung out of the saddle and knelt, lifting her head tenderly in his hand while feeling for a pulse with the fingers of his other. When it beat strong against his touch, he felt tears of gratitude sting his eyes. She was alive!

But looking at her, he wondered how she had managed to stay that way. Her robe was in tatters, and every inch of her skin was bruised and scratched.

Even in the driving rain and hail, her small feet ran blood. He quickly wrapped her in a blanket and urged Licorice homeward. The fight wasn't over yet.

Deirdre dreamed. Someone had made her warm. Toasty, even. She felt all floaty and comfortable. Nothing burned or froze or hurt.

She had died. That rushing dark shape coming at her out of the white hail had been Death. She gave a mental shrug. It hadn't hurt at all. Certainly no more than the agonies she had been through before. She had even had a sense of Sam's presence before the blackness took her. A sensation of his touch, of being lifted in his strong arms.

Death had been kind, but she felt a wrenching sadness that she would never again know that beloved presence or feel even the imaginings of his touch. She had been born to be his wife. Why had it all been taken from them both?

In spite of her comfortable state, she felt like crying. Sorrow for herself, but mostly for Sam. He had been left alive to deal with his loss, just as his own mother had been. She prayed that he wouldn't pine away as she had. That he would go on with his life, being the Guardian Angel to his town, his people.

It wasn't fair! They were *her* friends, her people, too. She had made a place in the community and would have made Sam a fine wife. Why couldn't she have survived to be the woman who would make his life complete. Feeling anger now, she forced her eyes open.

At first she couldn't focus. Then her eyes adjusted. God looked like her father. She glared at him.

"I wanted to marry Sam," she slurred. "Why didn't you let me?"

God looked amazed. "Deirdre?" he asked. "Can you hear me?"

"I asked a question, an' I wan' an answer!" She blinked, trying to keep the deity in focus.

"Deirdre, I . . ."

"I *love* him!" She closed her eyes and felt tears sliding down the sides of her face. "He loves me. You shouldnta done this."

Sam took Deirdre's face in his hands and gently shook her head. "It's the drug," he told the bewildered-looking senator. "I saw this in the service. Sometimes it makes the patient a little wacky."

"Wacky!" Andy commented from the driver's seat where he was pushing the Jeep at as high a speed as possible toward the Jackson hospital. "That shot of morphine you gave her has made the woman *stoned*."

"Shut up and drive," Sam warned.

"God!" Deirdre yelled, starting to thrash. Pain was returning to her body. Punishment for questioning? Then strong, familiar arms went around her. She gasped and opened her eyes.

Sam smiled down at her. "I couldn't give you too much morphine," he said. "Just enough to take the edge off. We'll be at the hospital soon, love. They can fix you up as good as new."

"Sam?" She stared at him. Living flesh. The real Sam. She wasn't dead! Then who . . .?

"Deirdre, you're going to be all right. You've had a horrible experience, but it's all over now, and if you want to marry Sam, you have all of my blessings.''

''Daddy?'' She turned and saw her father sitting beside her, a wide smile on his face. Taking in her surroundings, she realized fuzzily that she was in the back of the Jeep, that the rear seat had been lowered to make a flat area for her to lie on. The two men flanked her on either side, and she was wrapped in a cocoon of blankets.

And she hurt over every inch of herself. Deirdre started to laugh.

''Darling?'' Sam's voice held concern. She reached out and took his hand, squeezing weakly to reassure him.

''I'm okay, Sam,'' she said. ''I just never realized how terrific it was to hurt.'' He looked puzzled. ''It means I'm really alive,'' she explained.

''You thought you were . . .?'' Her father seemed unable to finish the question.

She laughed again. ''Yes. And, Dad, you'll never believe who I thought *you* were.'' Sam's laughter joined with hers as Richard Wilcox blushed.

SIXTEEN

Deirdre stayed in the Jackson hospital five days. Two, because she needed the care and rest to recover. Those she tolerated. The other three, she complained, were only because no one believed her when she declared that she was a bit stiff and sore but otherwise fine. Dr. Bennett told her she was a troublesome patient. Then he added that her powers of recuperation were remarkable, and on the fifth day, he freed her.

During the time she fretted in the confines of the hospital, she learned from Sam and her father that the three men who had conspired to abduct her were in custody and had been bound over in a federal court for trial. Her fire had forced the two who had actually taken her to flee southeastward right into the arms of a contingent of rangers and firefighters coming to control the blaze. They had been arrested on suspicion of starting the fire, but communications with the center the F.B.I. men had set up in the Lodge Pole station soon revealed who they really were.

Tad Browning had been in Lodge Pole, disguised and watching to make sure that his orders were carried out. The F.B.I. man who most closely resembled Sam had dressed in his clothes and had stayed in the station, acting as a stand-in. Senator Wilcox had handled the telephone conversations with Browning personally, persuading the reporter-turned-kidnapper that Deirdre was more important to him than to Sam, since she was his only child. Browning had seemed flattered by the attention from the man of political power but had foolishly allowed Richard to keep him on the phone long enough for Andy and the other agent to run a tap and locate him at a cabin just within the town limits.

"It all went very smoothly," Sam told her as he and Senator Wilcox drove her back to Lodge Pole. "There's only one matter unresolved now."

"Unresolved?" Deirdre frowned. She was seated beside Sam while her father rode in the backseat. She heard him chuckle.

"There's that little matter of your being so mad at not being allowed to marry this policeman of yours," Richard said.

Deridre turned. "I'm going to," she declared.

"Have you been asked?" Her father's eyebrows rose.

She looked at Sam's profile. Stoical, unexpressive, but there was the slightest twitch at the corner of his mouth, and she was certain that if she could look directly into his eyes, she'd see love for her. And amusement at her predicament.

"Well," she said. "No."

Sam drove on silently.

"Do you intend to do anything about that?" Richard asked, suppressed laughter clear in his deep voice.

"Yes. Sam, would you mind pulling over to the side of the road?"

Sam was having difficulty not stopping in the middle of the road and grabbing her in an embrace and asking her to marry him right then and there, but discussions with Richard Wilcox had made him wary of following his natural inclinations. The senator had explained about Deirdre's upbringing, how difficult it would be for her to be the one to "pop" the question, and that if she did, Sam could rest assured she meant it. So Sam waited.

"There's a pull-out about a quarter of a mile ahead," he said. "Good view of the mountains. Little chapel up the path toward the river. Haven't been in there for a while . . ."

"Drive us to the place," she said tightly.

Richard hummed softly, a contented sound, as they made their way to the turn-off, but otherwise silence was thick as Deirdre wrestled with her feelings.

She knew what was happening. These two wretches had gotten their heads together and planned to get her in the position of having to be the aggressor in the matrimonial issue. If for any reason in the future she had regrets, she knew she would only be able to blame herself. Sam and her dad would know that, too. Deirdre fumed.

But at the same time, she realized that she loved him so much that she would be able to adapt to his life. After the first week, she barely felt a pang of homesickness for the city, and that was even well before they were lovers. So what was the big deal?

She remembered how desperately she had desired one last look at his face when she thought that all was over for her.

Sam drove into the scenic look-out and stopped the car. "Care to take a little hike?" he asked, a gleam in those green eyes.

Deirdre stifled a sharp retort and got out of the car wordlessly. Richard got out, too, but said that he preferred to stay by the Jeep and enjoy the fantastic scenery. Deirdre looked up. It had been the first time that she had passed this section of road that she had not been looking at the mountains. Sam took her hand and started to lead her toward the small building that she realized was the chapel he had meant.

As they walked, holding hands, Deirdre felt all of the unease and awkwardness fall away from her. Sam's touch was a balm to her heart and soul, and she knew that she would easily be able to spend the rest of her life at his side. By the time they reached the door of the chapel, she was smiling.

Sam stopped and took both of her hands. "Care to share what's causing that smile?" he asked, gazing at her with love

Her smile widened, and she shrugged. "It's so simple, Sam. I love you, and I want to marry you."

He lifted one eyebrow. "You really think that a

popular Washington socialite who looks like she ought to be a Major Motion Picture Star will be happy with the humdrum life of—?"

"Humdrum! Listen, I've never lived through so much excitement in my entire life. And I hope I never have to again."

Sam enfolded her in his arms. "I hope so, too, Deirdre. I hope so, too. Let's go inside."

The interior of the small chapel was cool in contrast to the hot sunshine outside. Deirdre felt a peacefulness settle over her. And love grow. Sam put his arm around her shoulders.

"We'll get married, honey," he said, smiling down at her. "I can build onto my house. Add a few rooms. Maybe a nursery."

"Absolutely a nursery." She felt the love growing.

He bent and kissed her softly. "Look out at the mountains," he said, pointing to a large picture window at the altar end of the building. "They've been here for millenia. Our lives are like a gnat's by comparison, but I believe that you and I can be the best we can be *together*. Almost losing you made me realize how empty I'd be without you, love."

"I felt the same way," she admitted. "Maybe that's the reason the whole thing happened. So we'd *know*."

Sam drew her closer. "I knew quite some time ago," he admitted. "First felt it when you put on that cute little straw hat the day we were first in Jackson. I felt like that big old trout you had hooked."

"You did?" Her eyes were wide.

"Actually, I think I fell for you when I first saw

you." His lips touched her ear. "I was prepared to dislike you," he whispered, "because of the pressure brought on me to hire you. But I couldn't."

"You certainly made a good show of acting like it," she teased. "And then *firing* me."

"I thought you quit." Laughter was in his eyes.

"Oh, Sam." She threw her arms around his neck. "How soon can we do it?"

He nuzzled her neck. "There's a secluded meadow about a hundred yards away," he murmured. "I'm sure your dad won't mind a little longer wait."

"I mean *get married*, you sex fiend!"

"Oh, that." His lips closed over hers, stifling for a while any words she had to throw at him. Sam held her to him and tangled his fingers in the silky softness of her hair, a sense of exaltation rising in him. She was his and would soon be his wife forever!

By the time they returned to the Jeep, Richard was dozing in the backseat. He woke when they got into the front.

"Longest darned proposal I ever heard about," he said, humor in his tone.

"There were details to work out," Dierdre replied, aware that her hair was decorated with grass and leaves. She took a comb from her purse and began to groom away the evidence of the sealing of their agreement to matrimony with as much dignity as she could muster.

On the way into Lodge Pole, Sam explained to both Wilcoxes that he had talked to the town council about hiring another officer, a young man he had met down at the Law Enforcement Academy when he had guest-lectured there in the spring. "Although no one hopes for a repetition of this summer's events, I think it made the townspeople aware that they need more than two officers. Especially if one of them is going to be spending more time as a family man." He grinned.

"No more Guardian Angel?" Deirdre asked, genuinely surprised.

"I'm the chief," Sam declared. "Not some special supernatural protector who lives only to watch over the town. I think I harbored a few delusions of grandeur and allowed folks to feed those delusions." He reached for Deirdre's hand. "I have more to live for than just my job now. *Much* more."

"Hearing you say that erases any lingering doubts I was entertaining," Richard said. "I know a few people in law enforcement, and some of them do neglect their families out of an outsized sense of duty."

"Not this lawman." Sam squeezed the small hand he held. But he did it gently, as he had made love to her earlier. Very gently and tenderly, because she was still scarred from her flight through the forest. He knew some of the scars would never disappear completely, but he would love her all the more for them.

Deirdre looked down at the big hand covering hers. The scars that she had seen on it the first time they had met had faded. So would hers, inner and outer. But memory both in her skin tissue and in her mind would keep some of them visible for the rest of her life, reminding her how precious that life was and how much she wanted to live as long as she could with Sam. Returning to her old, self-destructive ways was now unthinkable. She would learn to be the most laid-back person in the world, she pledged herself.

Keeping that pledge proved a bit difficult over the next few weeks. Out of a sense of propriety, she moved back into the Thortons' home to live with her father while preparations for the wedding were made. Sam agreed to the arrangement, saying that he wanted to do a few things around his place that would make accommodating a wife more pleasant. They took time for horseback rides to secluded places for picnics and loving, but Sam didn't allow her into his home. Secret things, he said, were going on there. That, of course, piqued her curiosity, but Deirdre stayed away from the place.

Richard made arrangements to stay on, having his office relay anything he needed to act on and doing it by long distance. Deirdre could tell that he was both pleased and saddened, and she knew that she would miss him.

"But that's what airplanes and vacations are for," he told her. "Who knows, I might even get defeated next election and have nothing to do but come out here and bother you two." His blue eyes twinkled. "Of course, by then I hope there'll be more than two of you to visit."

Deirdre laughed and blushed. But after that she stopped taking her birth-control pills.

Sally and Martha Edwards took over as substitute mothers, Sally marshaling the festival details and Martha laboring over a wedding dress which Deirdre insisted on paying her for. Martha only took the price of the materials. The work, she declared, was out of friendship.

The evening before the ceremony, Sally closed the café and served a dinner for as many of Sam and Deirdre's friends as could crowd into the place. Then the men retired to one of the more sedate bars for a bachelor party organized by Andy. Try as she might, when her father finally dragged home, Deirdre could get no details of the festivities. He only smiled and commented that southerners weren't the only ones who knew how to throw good parties for a groom.

The morning of the wedding was crisp and clear, an ideal September day. Martha, Sally, and Julie spent the morning helping Deirdre prepare, while Richard disappeared to, as he put it, get a little more sleep because of the night before. Shaking his head as he went out the door, he muttered something about not being as young as he used to be.

Deirdre hoped that he and Sam would make it to the ceremony.

But Andy proved to be a reliable best man. Just an hour before they were supposed to meet at the church, he called her up and assured her that Sam was raring to go. "In fact," the younger man confessed, "he's in better shape than I am."

Deirdre did her own makeup but let Julie curl her hair into long golden ringlets. Sally and Martha helped her into the form-fitting, old-fashioned wedding dress, and when they fastened the veil over her hair and face, Deirdre could hardly believe it was herself she was seeing in the mirror.

"You're the prettiest bride this town's ever seen,"

Sally swore, looking at her proudly. Martha fussed with a fold in the skirt of the gown.

"Whatever I am," Deirdre said, a catch of emotion in her throat, "it's thanks to this town and to people like you." She gave each woman a hug and then asked to be alone for a minute. It was almost time for her father to pick her up for the drive to the church. The three left, giving her privacy.

Deirdre stood in the middle of the bedroom, thinking of all the events that had led to this moment. Each, it seemed, had been designed to bring her to the altar with Sam. Maybe she really did have a guardian angel. She heard her father coming in the front door and blinked back the tears that threatened to fall because of her emotions. It wouldn't do, she scolded herself, to smudge her makeup.

But Richard's eyes misted openly when he saw her. "You're as beautiful as your mother was, honey," he said, embracing her gingerly so as not to disturb the carefully arranged veil. "I only wish she could see you."

"Maybe she can," Deirdre whispered.

When they arrived at the church, the organist was already playing, and Richard gave her his arm. "Bye, honey," he said, looking at her. "In just a few minutes you won't be my little girl anymore. You'll be a married woman."

"Oh, Daddy." the tears threatened. "You know I'll always love you."

But when she saw Sam standing at the altar, waiting for her, she knew that no one would ever have her love in the special way that this man did. He was resplendent in a formal suit, his big, muscular frame dwarfing the other men around him. His black hair was neatly combed and gleamed in the sunlight that streamed in the church's windows. And when he saw her, his eyes blazed emerald.

Sam swallowed as she walked up the aisle toward him, her lovely face partly concealed by the veil. Never in all of his wildest fantasies had he imagined himself with a bride like her. His heart felt so full of love that he was almost dizzy.

The ceremony was mercifully quick, the minister an old friend who had realized that Sam needed it to be short, sweet, and binding. They exchanged simple gold rings, and after a few more words, the clergyman pronounced them husband and wife, telling Sam that he could kiss the bride.

His hands trembled slightly as he raised the veil. Deirdre's azure eyes were glimmering with tears, but the smile on her face told him that she was entranced in the same spell of joy that filled him.

Deirdre looked up at her husband. *I'm really married now,* she thought. Her life was now part of another's, one she loved beyond all understanding. She lifted her face as he lowered his head to kiss her. Dimly, she heard a collective sigh pass through the congregation, but mostly she was aware only of the loving caress of his lips on hers and the strong embrace of his arms, pulling her against his body. She was one with him.

But the townspeople were content to let them enjoy their first wedded kiss for only a short time. Soon there were goodnatured catcalls, hoots, and claims for kisses. Deirdre and Sam locked arms and ran down the aisle, only to escape into a shower of rice once they reached the comparative safety of outdoors.

Suddenly, Andy's voice, increased by the use of the department's bull horn, cut through the noise and laughter. There was, he announced, a surprise town party being thrown by the Edwards family and several other people who were close to Sam and Deirdre Cassidy. The location was the high school gymnasium, the only place big enough to hold everybody, and dance music was going to be provided by Tommy Edwards and a group of his friends. Food would be plentiful, he assured the crowd.

"Much as I'd like to start our own private party, wife," Sam said, looking down at her, "I guess . . ."

"I guess we shouldn't hurt our friends' feelings by not going," she finished, smiling. "I'm honored that they've gone to all this trouble."

"Me, too." Sam kissed her lightly.

It was the first of many light kisses she received that afternoon and evening. Only Andy dared his chief's wrath by giving her a good solid buss right on the mouth. Then he winked at her and declared that he'd been wanting to do that since he walked into the office that breezy day in late May and had seen her sorting through the litter on the station floor. "But now I got it out of my system," he assured Sam as he backed away from her.

Deirdre had to initiate a kiss with Tommy. His musical group was surprisingly good, and when they took a break, she went over to him and thanked him.

"I'm real glad you and the chief got hitched," Tommy said, blushing and ducking his head. "Hope someday I find a lady like you for myself.'' That was when she kissed him.

The party went on until late evening. But about eleven, Sam gave her a special look, and she nodded in response. She bid several people good night, thanking them for their help. For her father, she had a special word.

''I know you have to leave tomorrow,'' she said to him. ''But I want you to know how happy I am. Anytime you can manage it, please come here. We want to see you often.''

''I will, honey,'' Richard reassured her. He hugged her close and then gave her over to Sam.

''I wish we could have a proper honeymoon, sweetheart,'' Sam said as they drove home. ''But until the new man gets here and trained . . .''

''I don't need a honeymoon.'' Deirdre snuggled close to him. ''I just want to settle in and be your wife. No complications. No excitement.''

''Oh, there's going to be some excitement,'' he warned, and the tone of his voice made her start to tingle.

He parked the Jeep and hurried around to lift her into his arms directly from the passenger seat. Deirdre shivered in anticipation, and her curiosity surfaced again, wondering what he'd been up to in the house. When he led her across the threshold, she noted no major changes.

But when they entered the bedroom, she started to laugh until the tears came. Over the new king-size bed hung a wooden carving of outspread wings. Angel wings.

"Where did you get it?" she asked, hugging him tightly. "I've never seen a work quite like it."

Sam grinned. "Commissioned it from a friend who does woodwork in Jackson. It and the little mare waiting to meet you out in the corral with Licorice are my wedding presents to you."

Deirdre expressed her thanks with a passionate kiss. But then she started to laugh again. "I thought the days of the Angel were past," she said.

Sam walked over to the bed and laid her on it. He started to remove his suit. "You will notice, wife," he said, his tone seductive, "there is no halo with those wings."

Deirdre held open her arms for him. "Show me why, husband," she challenged. Sam Cassidy spent the rest of the night doing just that.